nextwave
agents of H.A.T.E.

THIS IS WHAT THEY WANT

WRITER: WARREN ELLIS
PENCILER: STUART IMMONEN
INKER: WADE VON GRAWBADGER
COLORIST: DAVE MCCAIG
LETTERERS: CHRIS ELIOPOULOS & VC'S JOE CARAMAGNA
ASSISTANT EDITOR: SEAN RYAN
CONSULTING EDITOR: MIKE MARTS
EDITOR: NICK LOWE

COLLECTION EDITOR: JENNIFER GRÜNWALD
ASSISTANT EDITOR: MICHAEL SHORT
SENIOR EDITOR, SPECIAL PROJECTS: JEFF YOUNGQUIST
VICE PRESIDENT OF SALES: DAVID GABRIEL
BOOK DESIGNER: CARRIE BEADLE
VICE PRESIDENT OF CREATIVE: TOM MARVELLI
EDITOR IN CHIEF: JOE QUESADA
PUBLISHER: DAN BUCKLEY

chapter
one
nextwave
healing America by beating people up.

Here are Elsa Bloodstone and The Captain, in Abcess, North Dakota.
So what made you want to be a super hero? Was it the clothes?
The mask, I guess.
Why?
So I could hit people in the face really really hard and run away and no one would know it was me.
What was your super hero name?
Captain ☠☠☠☠.
You're kidding me.
Nope. I was Captain ☠☠☠☠.
Why, for God's sake?
Hey, I'm from Brooklyn. I'm going to call myself Mr. Friendly? Hell, no. Captain ☠☠☠☠.
I met Captain America once. He asked me what my name was.
And you aid Captain ☠☠☠☠.
Man, he beat seven shades of it out of me. Left me in a dumpster with a bar of soap shoved in my mouth.
I was a bad super hero. Makes me wonder what I'm doing here, really.
Well, we're supposed to be checking out the site.
Yeah. I asked around.
They think that's a mall being built.
COFF

GAS
COFFEE
24
Well, hell, maybe the Beyond Corporation© ***will*** build a mall on it, once they've dug up whatever they think is under there.
Do we know what's under there?
Monica and Aaron say the document's unclear. Just that it's a buried biological weapon of mass destruction.
And they're excavating it to turn it into a working product.
If I have to bea up a lot of terrib little American proles today, I' absolutely goin to need more tea, darling.

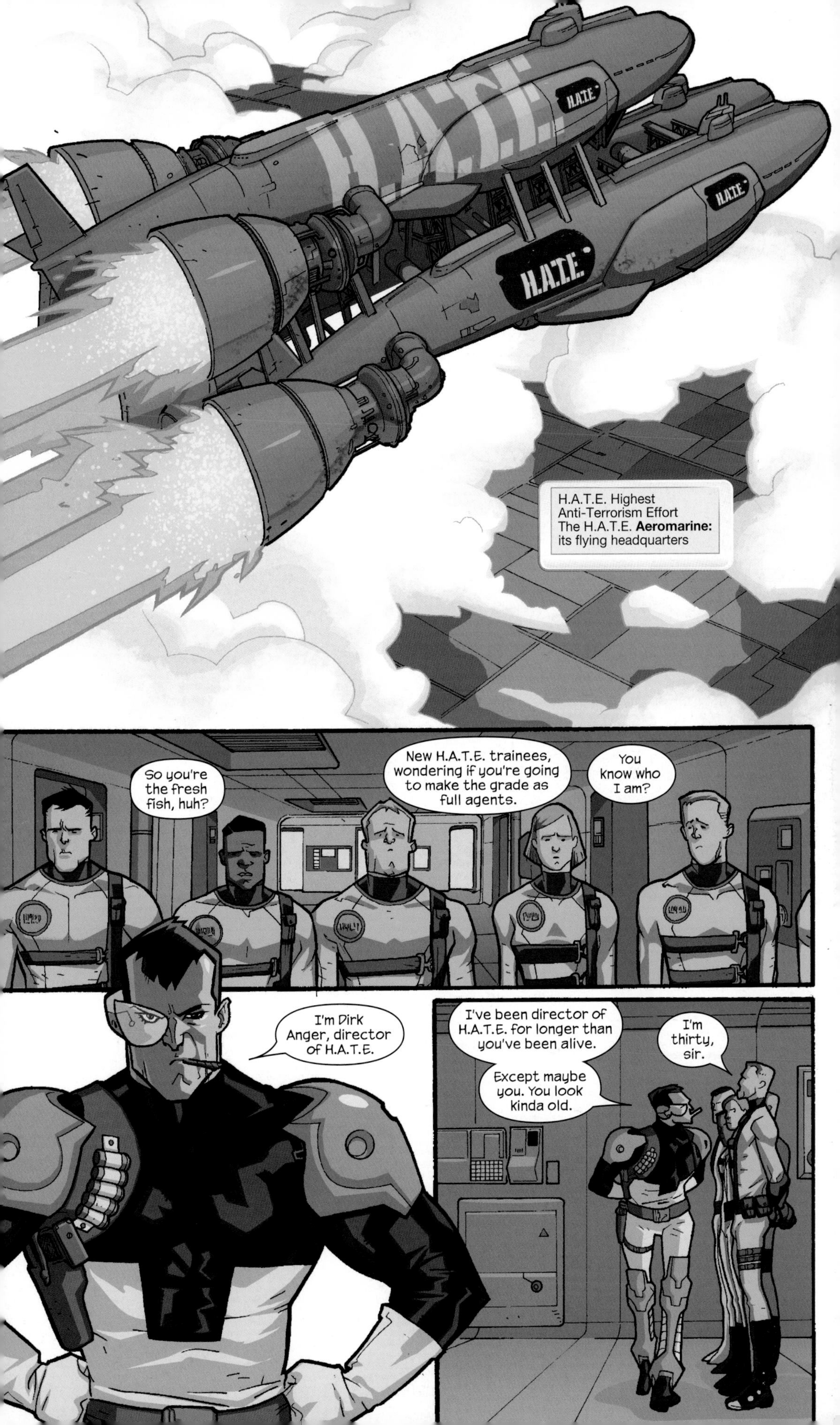
H.A.T.E.
H.A.T.E.
H.A.T.E.
H.A.T.E.
H.A.T.E. Highest Anti-Terrorism Effort The H.A.T.E. **Aeromarine:** its flying headquarters
So you're the fresh fish, huh?
New H.A.T.E. trainees, wondering if you're going to make the grade as full agents.
You know who I am?
I'm Dirk Anger, director of H.A.T.E.
I've been director of H.A.T.E. for longer than you've been alive.
Except maybe you. You look kinda old.
I'm thirty, sir.

Thirty? You look like a bag of dried buttskin.
I'm older'n you. I'm ninety years old. You know how I look so pretty? I take drugs.
Special H.A.T.E. drugs. Life-extending drugs.
H.A.T.E. has the best drugs. Because H.A.T.E. loves me.
And I love H.A.T.E.
Every day of my horrible drug-extended terrorist-fighting life.
Every day I smoke two hundred cigarettes and one hundred cigars and drink a bottle of whisky and three bottles of wine with dinner.
And dinner is meat.
Raw meat.
The cook serves me an entire animal and I fight it bare-handed and tear off what I want and eat it and have the rest buried.
In New Jersey!
For H.A.T.E.!
General Anger, we've located the Shockwave Rider again.
Okay. Communications room.

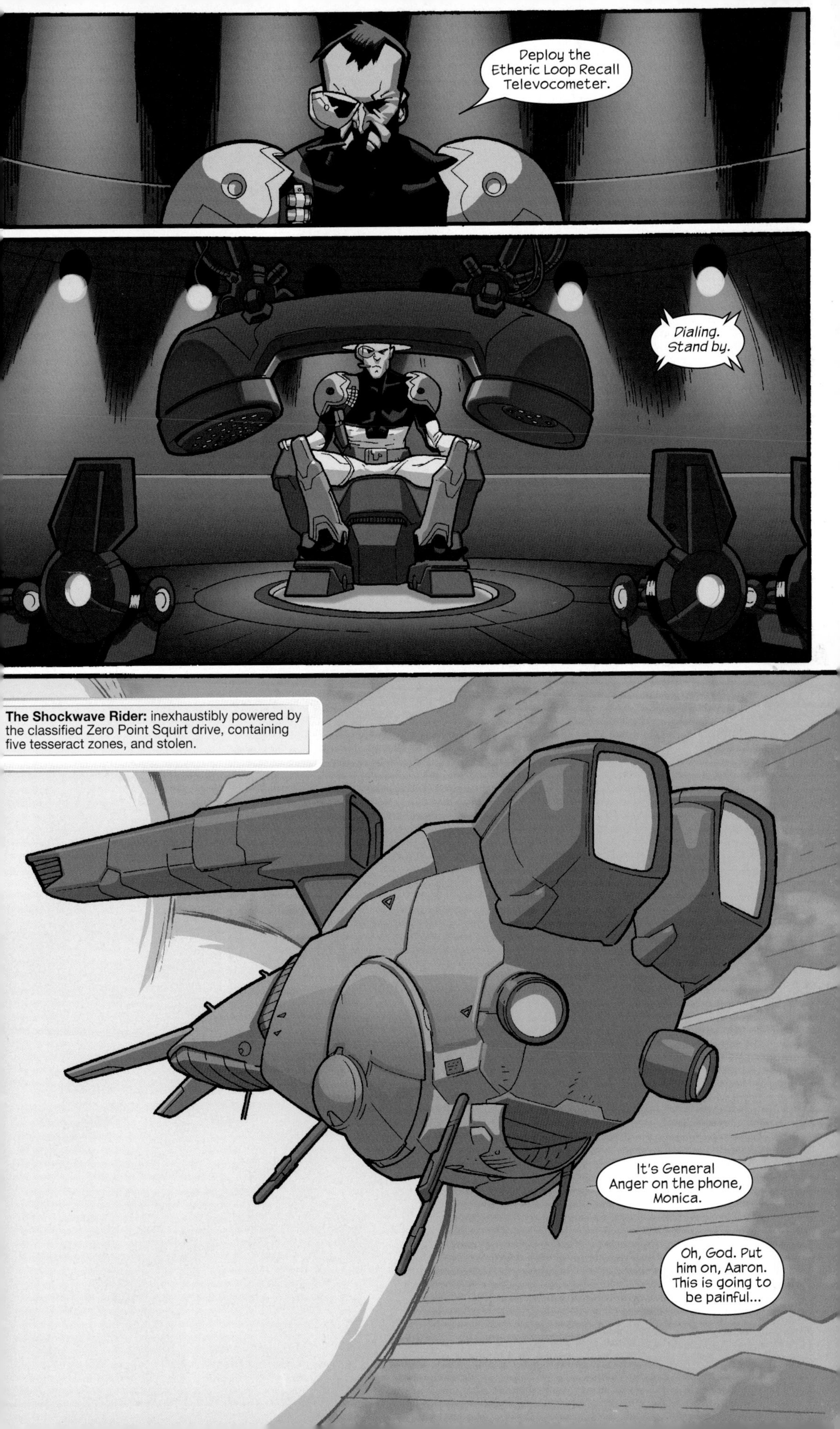
Deploy the Etheric Loop Recall Televocometer.
Dialing. Stand by.
The Shockwave Rider: inexhaustibly powered by the classified Zero Point Squirt drive, containing five tesseract zones, and stolen.
It's General Anger on the phone, Monica.
Oh, God. Put him on, Aaron. This is going to be painful...

Dirk. It's Monica.
Miss Rambeau. Please return to the Aeromarine with the highly classified experimental aircraft you and your team saw fit to steal while abandoning your posts.
Dirk. Here's the thing.
You hired us as your elite anti-terrorism team. The Nextwave Squad.
But you're getting your funding and technology from the Beyond Corporation©.
It was an open bidding process!
Faith-based funding!
The Beyond Corporation is what S.I.L.E.N.T. turned into.
You remember S.I.L.E.N.T., Dirk.
S.I.L.E.N.T. was a terrorist cell.
...that's an oversimplification of the actual situation.
Dirk, we found the Beyond Corporation©'s Marketing Plan.

s a blueprint for using H.A.T.E. and
ir own resources to product-test
sual Weapons of Mass Destruction
on the American public.
And get payment and political power for doing it.
We're not supporting that, Dirk. We told you all this already. It's why we left.
Please come back?
Kill the line, Aaron.
Yes. Silence, fleshy one.
Aaron. I understand the whole Robot Pride thing, but I've asked you not to call humans "fleshy ones".
Ah. Sorry.
It's okay, it's just...it's creepy, okay?
Monica Rambeau is a veteran super hero, previously known as Captain Marvel, whose mother always wanted her to get a proper job. So she joined H.A.T.E.
When her mother died, she went to Hell, and is used as a bucket by giant weasels dressed as cheerleaders. And that's what happens when you tell your kids to get a proper job.

nextwave

warren ellis*writer* **stuart immonen***penciler*
wade von grawbadger*inker* **dave mccaig***colors*
chris eliopoulos*letterer* **sean ryan***assistant editor*
mike marts*consulting editor* **nick lowe***editor*
joe quesada*editor in chief* **dan buckley***publisher*

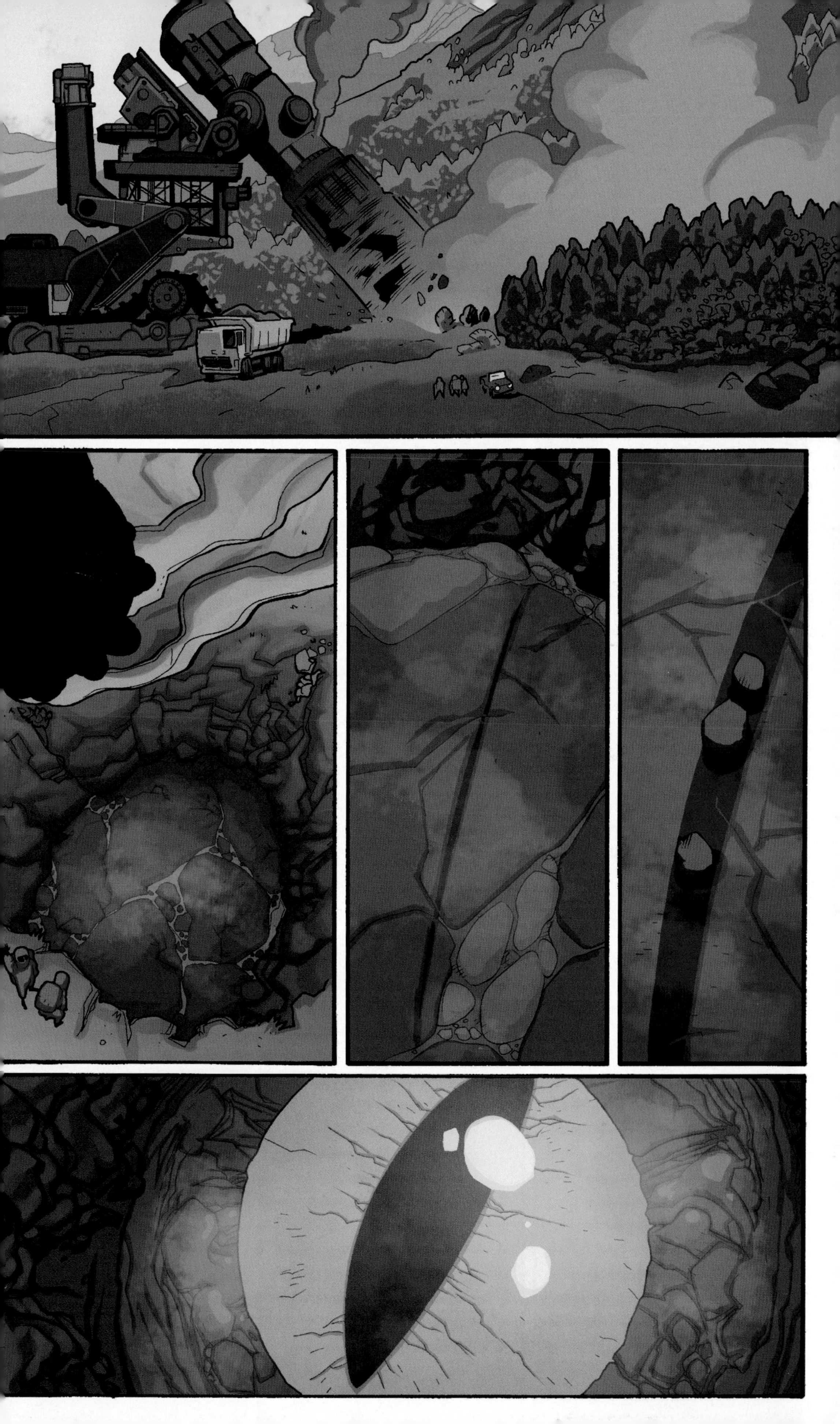

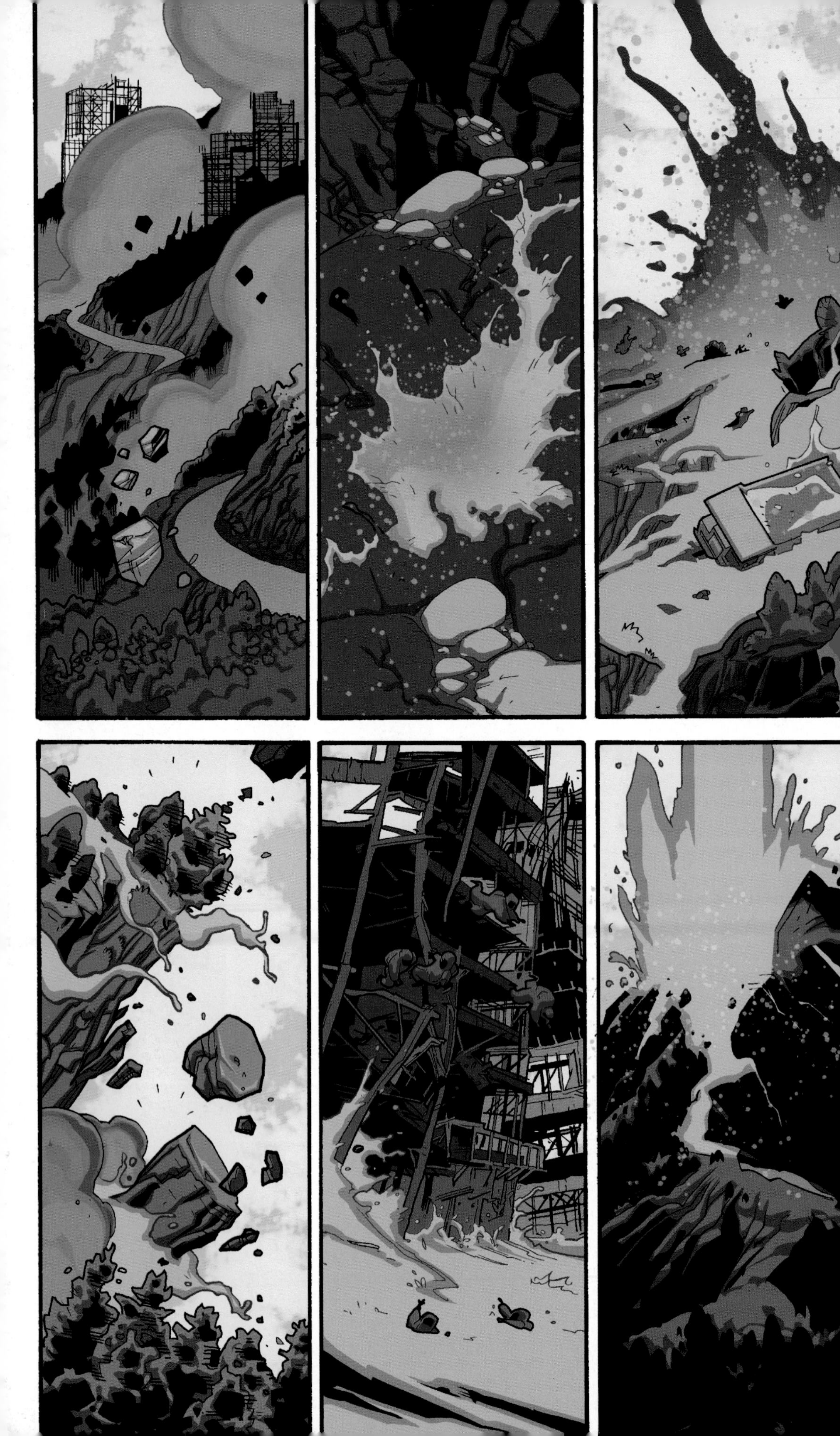

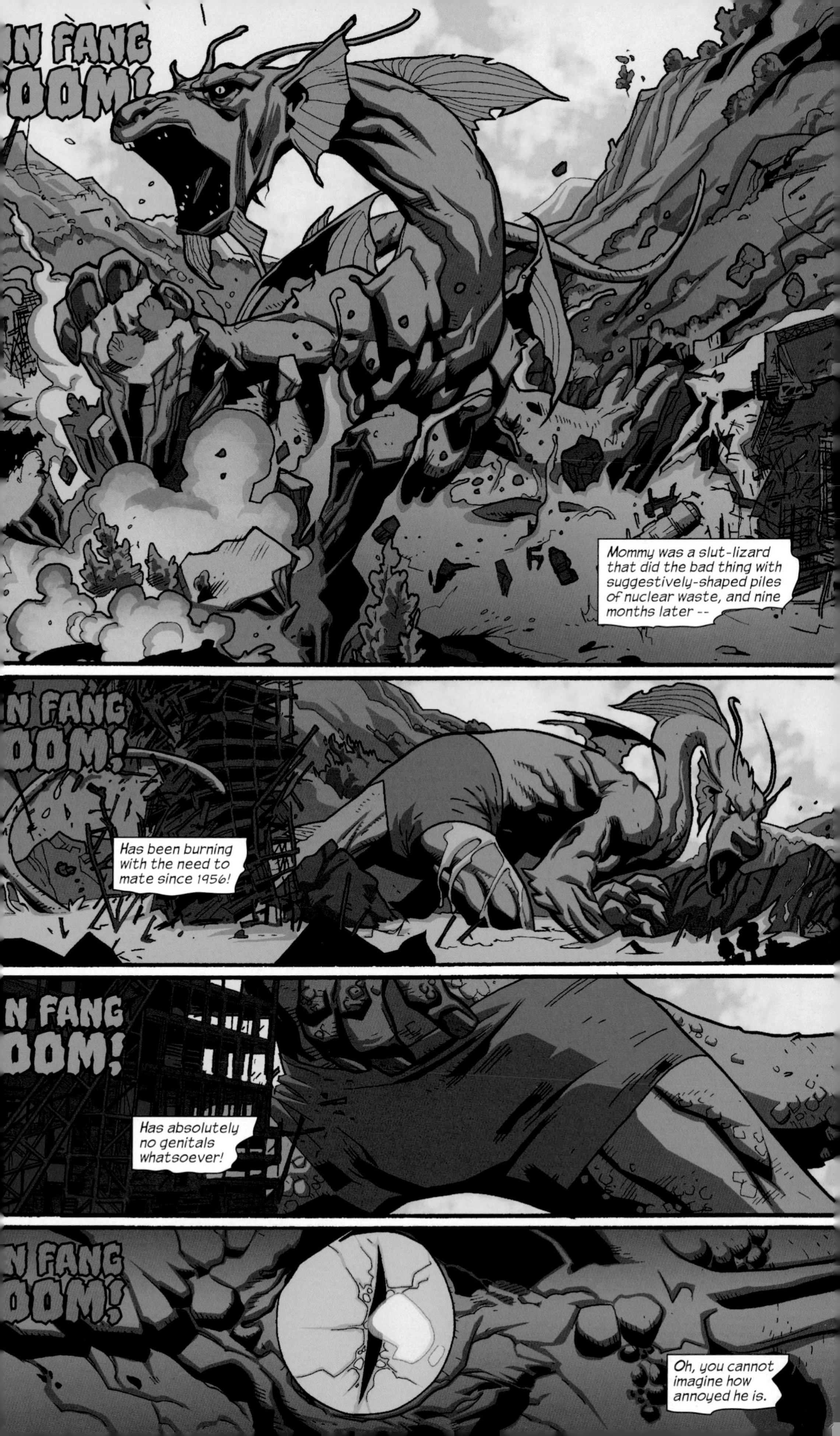

N FANG OOM!
Mommy was a slut-lizard that did the bad thing with suggestively-shaped piles of nuclear waste, and nine months later --
N FANG OOM!
Has been burning with the need to mate since 1956!
N FANG OOM!
Has absolutely no genitals whatsoever!
N FANG OOM!
Oh, you cannot imagine how annoyed he is.

is a super hero comic about five people wh
have just minutes to prevent a town from
being eaten by a giant lizard monster.
In purple underpants.

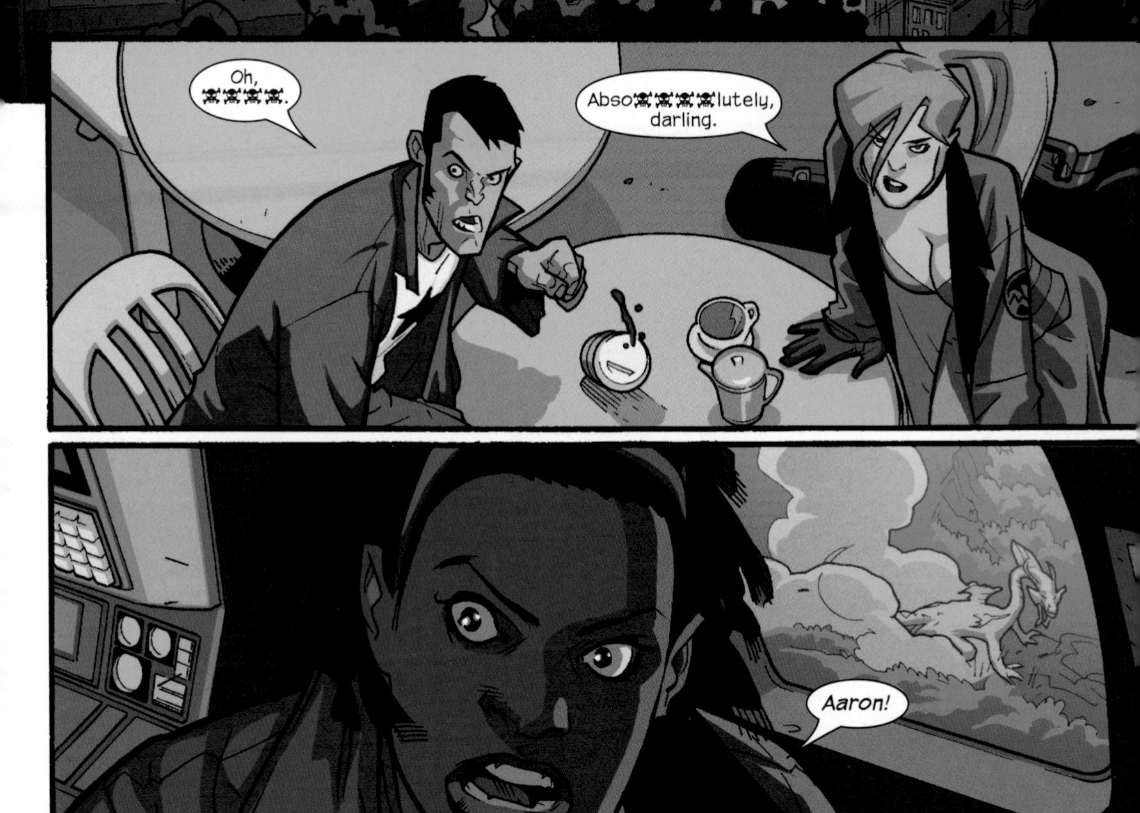

My robot brain needs beer.
There's beer in there?
I wish. Just saying. I'm hooked into the hull cameras, I know what's down there. I've called Tabby.
uldn't we be using enames? Maybe I hould be calling you--
Machine Man? My name's Aaron Stack. Aaron is fine.
In the Avengers, we all had codenames. Maybe we should keep them.
What's the point? Besides, do you really want to keep your super hero name?
"Photon" doesn't strike fear into the hearts of men, surely.
"Hello. I am a tiny insignificant particle. Put down your guns or I'll bounce off of you undetectably."
The Captain kept his codename.
The Captain can't remember his real name. Ellie Bloodstone never had a codename. Tabitha has had about nine.
And they all sucked!
I was on the phone when you called. What's the problem?

Put that on. Personal flight harness. We're going live.
There's something here? The Marketing Plan I stole was right?
Yeah. There's something here, it's a hundred and fifty feet tall, and it's probably going to eat the town.
Why do I need to fly?
Because if you fight on the ground you'll get trodden on.
Isn't that English girl fighting on the ground?
Yeah, but she annoys me.
Let's go to work.

DWARD
MUSIC
Ellie, hold on--
No! Go take care of Lizard pants! I can handle this!
Don't argue with me, or it's the Kenyan Nipple Torture for you again!
I'm going, I'm going...
MUSIC S
Damn.
Okay. This'll do.
I FIRE YOU WITH BULLETS NOW.

Come on then, if you think you'r hard enough.
I said *come on!* Don't *bore* me, you horrid little men.
BITE MY CORDITE, LANKY.
Oh, *yes!*
Well *played,* you disturbing metal-faced object you.

I shall kick you to death with slippers on, so it doesn't hurt so much.
I'm an awful liar, aren't I, darling?
OWW!
Sod.
NO NO NOT DOING THIS NO NO NO RUN AWAY RUN AWAY THIS IS MY SPECIAL RUN AWAY SONG SO I DO NOT GET KILLED BY SCARY GIRL.

Do **not** run away from me.
BEYOND
CORPORATION
HUMAN RESOURCES DEPARTMENT

Aaron? Ellie. Tell Monica--Beyond© knows we're here.
I've just been attacked by some freaks badged as their Human Resources Department, of all things.
We're fighting a war on two fronts.
Lucky I brought my babies, sweetie.
Did you kill them? When I ran The Avengers--
Oh, here we go...
--when I ran the Avengers, we didn't kill people, Elsa.
Did Monica always hold all life sacred?
YAPYAPYAP
YAPYAPYAP
YAPYAPYAPYA
YAPYAPYAPYA
YAPYAP YIP

Bad doggie go sizzle pop.
Monica!
They're not people.
...hm?
Two arms, two legs, bad suits. They might be pretty crappy people, but they're people.
Darling, you may have run the Avengers, but I come from a line of near-immortal monster hunters, and I know a non-human when I kill it.
Remote scanning...she's right. Those humanoids were grown, probably on slabs of genetically modified kelp.
They move lik people, but the missing a bunc organs, and mo of their brain
In fact, they'r wearing softwa Beyond Corpora Fightpersona X in fact.
Plant-based robots driven by a computer operating system.
But they're alive, right?
Depends on your definition of alive They have more i common with brocc than they do wit you. Or me.

I hate broccoli. Let's kill 'em.
But first: the Beyond Corporation© has woken up a giant lizard and don't seem to be controlling it too well.
Tabby: go tame a monster.
Tabitha Smith possesses the **mutant powers** of **blowing things up** and **stealing all your stuff.**
tick tick tick
Boom.

Oh my God.
It's wearing underpants.
you have been reading
nextWAVE

LIVE GILL ON GRILL ACTION
FIN FANG FOOM
VS
MACHINE MAN
"I WEAR UNDERPANTS"
"MY NAME'S AARON STACK"
NEXTWAVE
ETS THEIR LOVIN' FROM YOUR MAMA!
NOT ON TV
LOSED CIRCUIT
BONUS FIGHT!
chapter two
ELSA BLOODSTONE VS. BROCCOLI MEN!

Why do giant monsters eat people?
Human beings are mostly water. Their tissues and fluids retain flavors and other residues from their food. Their bones have a brittle quality. Their skin is warm and pliant.
Thirst-quenching, well-seasoned, crunchy and yet chewy: People are the Elvis of snack food.

y **Smith** is here with
t was the Nextwave
d to make the giant
onster go away.
FIN FANG FOOM PUT YOU IN HIS **PANTS.**

NOOOOOOO!
Hold on.
He's going to put me in his pants!
I heard. Get ready to jump.
The Captain is so absurdly strong that he once smacked someone's spine out through their lungs just by patting them on the back.
In his defense, he was quite extraordinarily drunk.

AAAAOOOOOOOOOOO

Ouch.
The pants might have been less painful.
You're welcome.
We need a better plan than this. Unless you think we can take him by breaking his fingers.
Maybe Monica has a plan. After all--
--she used to run the Avengers.
You think she gets tired of telling people that?
I'm damn sure I get ☠☠☠☠ tired of hearing it.
☠☠☠☠ yeah.

H.A.T.E. Aeromarine
ing aimlessly above
North America...
I hate Monica Rambeau. I should never have let girls into such a sensitive part of the organization.
Dirk Anger, Director Of Highest Anti-Terrorism Effort: Formed and employed the Nextwave Squad, until they went piratey.
I hate girls.
General Anger?
Girls have soft bits. Agents of H.A.T.E. shouldn't have soft bits.
They should have hard bits.
Muscles and stuff.
I have hard bits.
Yes, General Anger.
I do.
Lots of them.
I think I'm having a nervous breakdown.
Yes, General Anger.

The following dialogue is coming from inside this thing, which is bigger on the inside than it is on the outside. Thank you.
Hull cameras have just picked up Tabby and the Captain being smacked through a building.
What?
The Captain took the brunt the impact. The probably bot still alive.
Okay. Put this thing into a parking orbit and then follow me in.
nextWAVE
warren ellis writer stuart immonen penciler
wade von grawbadger inker dave mccaig colors
vc's joe caramagna letterer sean ryan assistant editor
mike marts consulting editor nick lowe editor
joe quesada editor in chief dan buckley publisher

onica Rambeau can onvert part or all of her nass into any form of ectromagnetic energy the spectrum. Except the ones they make up on *Star Trek*.
Right. Let's see if I can remember how to do this.
Exawatt gamma-ray laser--

What the hell? That would've skewered anything else...
HEY!
I can't even blow his bloody toenails off!
Tell me about it. I thought maybe this might go differently.
Well, it's gone bloody pear-shaped is what it's gone!
Stop whining, girl. We're not done yet.
Here we go--Brothers and sisters, I have a scheme...
Oh, shut up.
This really bloody hurts my arm, by the way.

Okay, so we can't break its hide. So we need a new plan.
Lateral thinking.
Is that what they taught you in the Avengers? That and beware of spooky chicks who think they've been made pregnant by robots?
I could make you pregnant.
I am full of very useful devices.
Not unless you could do it from over there, clanky.
...yes. Yes, you are.
You're a little old for me.
Shut up. I have a plan.
We're going to make lizard breath swallow you.
What?
We're going to get you inside that thing.
I hate you, fleshy one.
More of those Human Resources freaks on the way.
Yeah. They want a full test on that thing's destructive capabilities, so they need us out of the way.
You, me and Tabby will keep them busy. Ellie, you're going to make beastie open his mouth for Aaron.

How?
I don't care.
I'm keeping my special Avengers' training to myself until you start being nicer to me.
Here it comes...
Okay, okay, I heard, how do I do this, okay...
...oka Got i Aaron, read
What's she doing?
Follow her, for God's sake. We're busy.

EEEEEEEEEEEEEE
DEATH TO FLESHY ONES!

Sorted.
Tick tick tick

Boom!
Microwave Storm!

Kick!
'Splode!
next
THIS IS WHAT THEY WAN

Aaron Stack, designation X-51 from Dr. Abel Stack's self-built sequence of sentient humanoid combat robots. It is not known what happened to the other fifty.
I make you die with steamy electric mek bits now clack clack clack.
More tea, Father?
...confirmed.
Father... are you crying?
Father Blood Drench Robo Crush simply has something in his lens.
Leave Father Blood Drench Robo Crush alone now, fleshy.

Biological systems are hideous.
I can't believe they have all this garbage inside them and not want to kill themselves.
Aaah, joy. The stink of digesting humans.
Time to work.

FIN FANG OOM'S EYES URT REALLY A LOT!
Damnit, Monica. Lizard pants is still wrecking the place. Your robot's rubbish.
He's not my robot.
Okay--the robot who follows us around and stares at my chest is rubbish.
Well, he's all we've got.

HURK
FIN FANG FOOM
NEEDS
BATHROOM
FIN FANG FOOM...EAT TOO MANY PEOPLE...?
Public Parking

RUN--FOR YOUR LIFE!
FIN FANG FOOM'S... HEART...?
FIN FANG FOOM'S HEART...
...IS BROKEN...

My robot brain needs beer.
Also? I want to die.

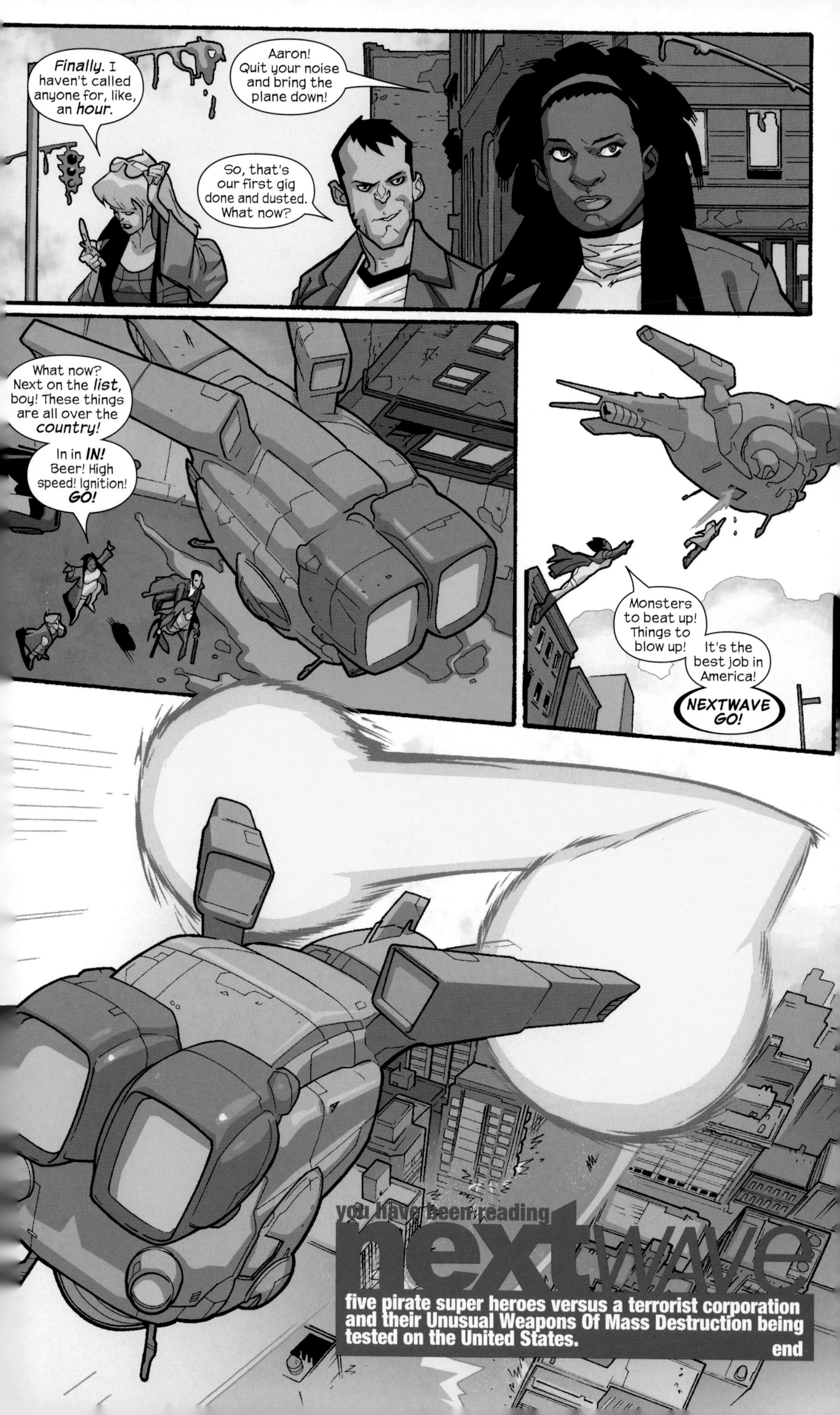

Finally. I haven't called anyone for, like, an hour.
Aaron! Quit your noise and bring the plane down!
So, that's our first gig done and dusted. What now?
What now? Next on the list, boy! These things are all over the country!
In in IN! Beer! High speed! Ignition! GO!
Monsters to beat up! Things to blow up!
It's the best job in America!
NEXTWAVE GO!
you have been reading
nextWAVE
five pirate super heroes versus a terrorist corporation and their Unusual Weapons Of Mass Destruction being tested on the United States.
end

chapter
three
NEXTWAVE
AGENTS OF H.A.T.E.
immonen.ca 05

hird Precinct
ink City, Illinois:
Monday
Last week on the beat, Mangel?
Yep. One more week, then I spend the rest of my life rotting in a lounger.
Must be nice.
Yeah, well.
I earned it.

Mac.
Officer Mangel.
What did I tell you about dealing here?
Did you think I was going soft in my last week?
I said I still wanted my cut!
Officer!
Hm?
I can hardly see-- you're a police officer, right?
Sure, why not. What seems to be the problem?
I've been mugged! They got my wallet. Thank God I keep my billfold in my pants pocket--
They didn't get your billfold?

No, I keep them separate, always seemed safer--
Very clever of you, sir. Please step this way.
Okay...
1st Floor- Molly (dancer)
2nd Floor- Eve (schoolteacher)
3rd Floor- Anna (actress)
Mangel.
Here to see the girls.
They're waitin' on you.

Last week on the job, huh, Mangel?
Yeah.
Well, you can go on out and find someone to terrorize at the old folks' home. We're done.
We're done when I say we're done, Eve.
Like hell.
And you just used up your one chance, Mangel.
I been waiting to do you like a chicken for the pot since I met you.
EEEEEEEEEEE

Two things.
One: I want my ☠☠☠☠ cut. Now.
Two: clean his blood and snot off my boot.

Whassat?
Someone there?
I can hear you moving. Come on out.
MOW
RRRP
C'mere, little guy...
C'mon... I bet I can sell you...
What the hell are you?

nextWAVE
arren ellis*writer* stuart immonen*penciler*
ade von grawbadger*inker* dave mccaig*colors*
s joe caramagna*letterer* sean ryan*assistant editor*
ke marts*consulting editor* nick lowe*editor*
quesada*editor in chief* dan buckley*publisher*

H.A.T.E.
Highest Anti-Terrorism Effort
Director General Dirk Anger's
Private Armory Test Range
NO ENTRY UNDER ANY CIRCUMSTANCES
NO GIRLS
General?
I'm busy...
General, it's about the Nextwave Squad.
This really isn't a good time.
They've been spotted in the skies over western Illinois.
If they're hunting down whoever receive
the Seed, we have a viable windo
to intercept and capture them.
CLICK
I'm so alone.

Sink City: Wednesday
So I was in the Hyperlounge on Sunset? Like a block down from the Standard?
So I was in the Hyperlounge and it was all cool?
Jessica had passed out and Paris was hitting on this Italian guy with platinum eyes?
And this guy comes up to me and says you're all hot and stuff?
And I tell him, you know, dude, I totally *know*.
And he's all like, come to the men's room with me.
So--no, yeah--so I go to the men's room with him, and all of a sudden he's all like breathing funny and taking his clothes off.
And I'm just, you know, whatever. And he's all, you will *lurve* me now.
And he's got a costume on underneath his clothes. Like a super hero suit?
And he's like, you are Tabby Smith and you are my super hero wife now.
I KNOW!
Like I'm gonna--yeah, no--you should've *seen* the costume!
Girl, it was a color that *not even actresses* would be seen in.

Huh.
I'm gonna call you back.
No, I'm supposed to be, like, looking for something? Yeah. Laters.
UURRRRRR

tick tick tick
BOOM!

FASTER PUSSYCAT KILL KILL KILL
KILL KILL KILL
KIIIIIIILLL
I said BOOM.

Monica? I think I saw your guy, but he got away.
And Human Resources is already on the scene.
How did I know he was our guy? He was like twelve-feet tall and eating a car.

OWWW
Oh, ☠☠☠☠.
Everybody out!
You're the big-time monster hunter--you're volunteered.
One of us needs to keep looking for whoever's got the thing inside him--

have
ght an episode of
nextWAVE
unless you stole it off the Internet
Everyone get down on the deck *NOW!*

Welcome to the worst day of your life.

Help! I just lost the use of my right arm!
Where's Ellie?
WOO HOOOO!
Mommy
DEATH RACE 2000!
I AM PRESIDENT FRANKENSTEIN!
Where's the English ☠☠☠☠ going?
Off to hunt the guy you lost.
We figure a twelve-foot guy won't be hard to spot--especially for the big-deal monster-hunting English ☠☠☠☠.

SHOES
ALSACE
Drive on the proper side of the road, Colonial scum!
That's it, Yanks--make way for Miss Bloodstone!
Miss Bloodstone is in control.
Now, if I were some poor sod who'd been accidentally implanted with something called an Ultra Samurai Seed that the Beyond Corp Marketing Plan didn't fully explain--
--I'd stay off the main roads, wouldn't I?
And, from what little we know--
--I'd be hungry. I'd need to feed the change.
Sink City Very Small School With Lovely Children Inside

Munchies.
Oh, you are ☠☠☠☠ winding me up.
AAAAA!

Whassat?
This is a gas tank.

You're going home in the back of an ambulance.

Uurrrrr
When I kill you with a motor-car, you should have the common decency to stay dead, you horrid little object.
HA HA HA HA HA HA
He will peel you wit his robot bits.
you have been reading
nextwave
a comic single about five pirate super heroes twisting the nipple of the military-industrial complex. To be continued...

nextwave
agents of H.A.T.E.
chapter four
THE CAPTAIN
NOT REALLY A CAPTAIN OF ANYTHING
immonen.ca 05

This is **Mac Mangel**, a bad policeman whose body was invaded by a strange metal thing and is now eating things to feed it.

"Things" definitely include small children.

This is **Ellie Bloodstone.** She's just run Mac Mangel over with a jeep and then shot its gas tank to explode its fuel on top of him.

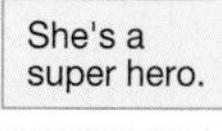

This is
nextWAVE

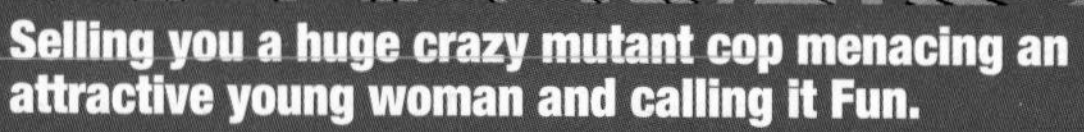

Selling you a huge crazy mutant cop menacing an
attractive young woman and calling it Fun.

EEEEEEEE!
EEEEEEEEEEEE!

Looked like a flare-gun shot.
It kind of was. Modified flare round. Ever since we found out these guys are half-broccoli, I've wanted to know if they'd burn.
Where's the guy?
A few blocks over.
He landed in a bunch of cars at like three hundred miles an hour. He's not getting up.
Cap! That was the guy! You left him there?
Oh my God. I blew him up with a jeep and he was still going. How stupid are you?
The Origin Of The Captain:

Well, Spa-Fon. We have looked everywhere.
Indeed, Squa-Tront. We have walked across this hellish landscape, and found no one.
Surely there must be one person to whom we can gift the Messianic Siddha-complex.
One person we can grant great powers to, that they may rescue their fellows from this terrible environment.
(Singing a truly filthy song by the Sex Pistols)
A fine young human specimen.
Young man. We come bearing the gift of super-human abilities beyond your mortal Ken.
Leprechauns. Cool.
Youth, we offer you magical powers with which to make this nightmarish land of "Brooklyn" a better place.
Yeah? Where?
Here. The heartstar of the space between galaxies.

This.
That's it?
Indeed. You are empowered, young man. Go forth and do great things.
I thought maybe it'd be like a thing that I could, you know...sell.
This is just ☠☠☠☠.
We have granted you mightiness and glory.
Huh.
I thought when you hit leprechauns on the head they turned into gold coins.
What a rip.

I wonder if they got credit cards.
HOOAAAAARRRKKKK
Oh boy.
Bending over was a *baaad* move.
I'm not stupid.

YOU'RE ALL UNDER ARREST.
nextWAVE
warren elliswriter stuart immonenpenciler
wade von grawbadgerinker dave mccaigcolors
vc's joe caramagnaletterer sean ryanassistant editor
mike martsconsulting editor nick loweeditor
joe quesadaeditor-in-chief dan buckleypublisher
Okay, so I'll fix it.
Giant unkyard robot. How hard can it be?

Oh, c'mon.
Seriously.
Wha--
OW!

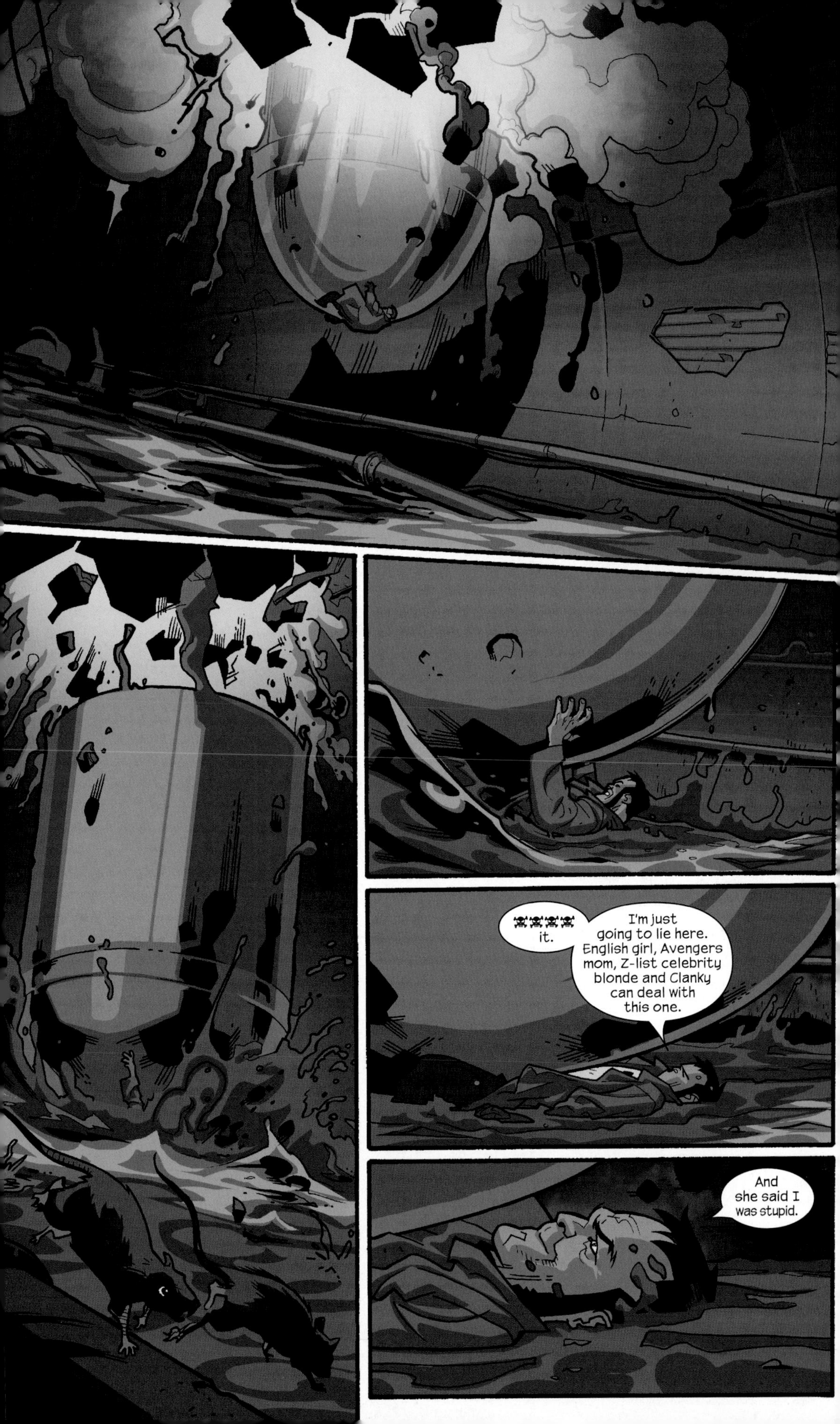
☠☠☠☠ it.
I'm just going to lie here. English girl, Avengers mom, Z-list celebrity blonde and Clanky can deal with this one.
And she said I was stupid.

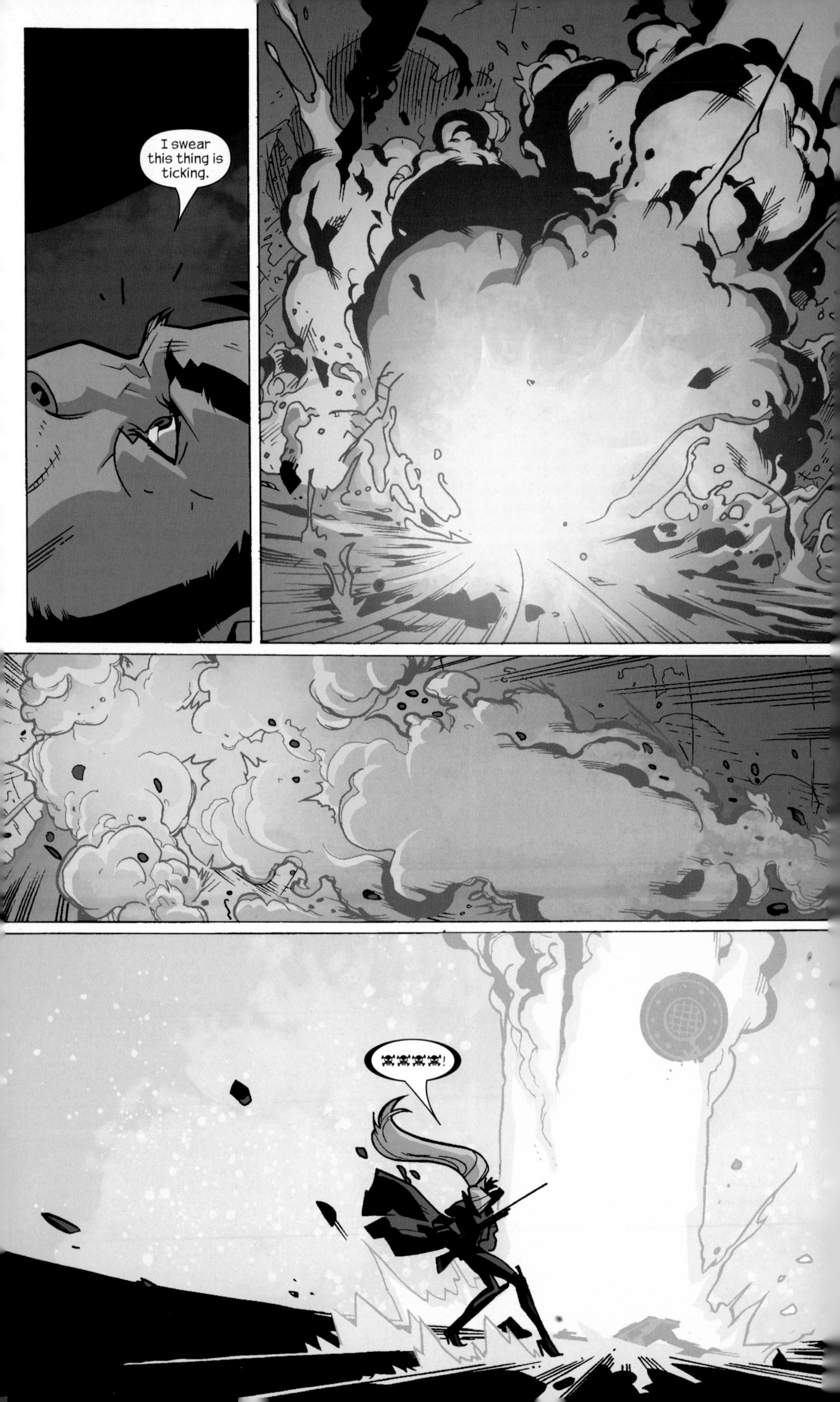
I swear this thing is ticking.
☠☠☠☠!

Oh, hell. Now what?
Get up, Monica. You have to, you know, tell us what to do.
She's not moving.
Monica! Quick! Captain America just called to invite you back to the Avengers!
...nothing.
She must be unconscious.

I'LL SHOW THEM.
I'LL SHOW THEM ALL.
What exactly is happening here? He wasn't that big before.
Can you, like, look inside him?
Sure.
Oh, God.
What?
Does that impress the robot girls or something?
Okay, he's inside it. And there's something inside him.
The thing is building around him.
Ultra Samurai seed, Monica said.
That's what the marketing plan called it. What if the Beyond Corporation released something into the wild...
...a parasite that made its host turn into a giant robot warrior? Using whatever metal was lying around?

Huh. Okay. Let me have a look.
Hey!
Oh, I see now. Okay. This is easy. Back me up.
Where re you joing?
I'm gonna kill me a giant robot.
Killing obots is *sick!*
I AM THE LAW!
GIMME YOUR WALLETS!
Get out of my way! Super hero coming through!

HA HA, CUTE GIRL.
LITTLE LOVE FOR A COP? HAH? HAH?
You want to date me?
Get naked.

Tick tick tick.
BOOM.

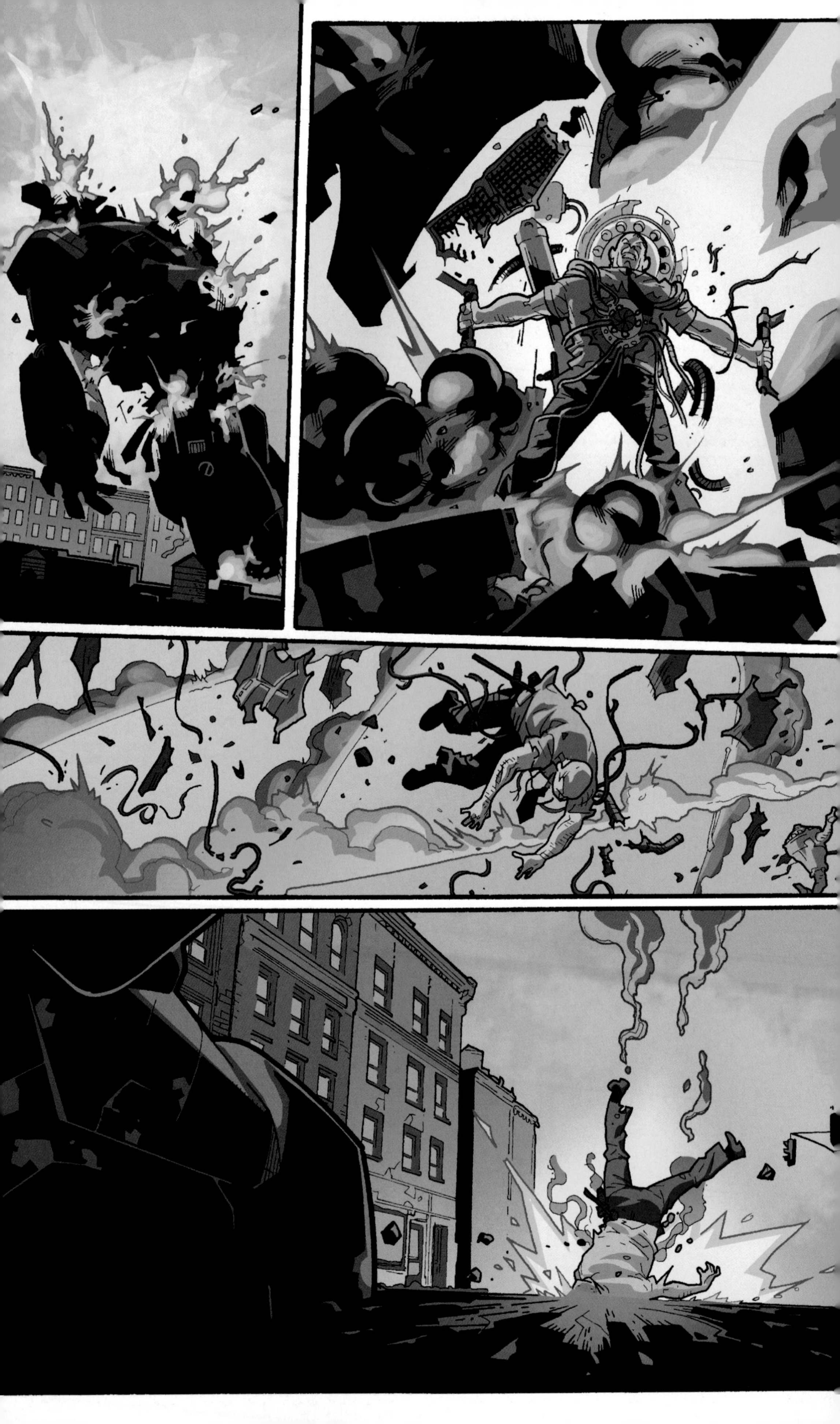

meep
meep
Awwww.
Cuuuute.
Die anyway.
And as for *you*...

P--
P--
Police.
Oh, man. You're a cop?
You're kidding me!
Cop.
I hate cops!
Uugg...
Because, like, cops keep arresting me and stuff? For stealing?
Like stealing's a crime or something?
Hey! What's going on?
He's a cop, Aaron!
Cops--the most annoying fleshy ones of all.

Tabby! Aaron!
What the hell are you doing?
Beating up a cop.
My God! That's a police officer! Get away from him!
But he--
Police! Officer! We do not beat on police officers!
This is you, isn't it, Aaron? Just another fleshy one to you?
But--
I don't want to hear it! Bring the Shockwave Rider down!
Are you all right, sir?
Kah
Ffah
He'll be fine.

We'll look after him.
Yeah. We're his *friends.*
There you go. Good cops can always rely on the community.
Nuuuh...
My dad used to say it takes special people to understand that police officers are the servants of the society.
You'll be fine with these people. The nightmare is over, officer.
Pppplease...
Noooooo...
Oh, yeah.
You'll be fine with us.
Now, what d'you want to be first? Our old lady or our restroom?
Or do you just wanna *die?*

What exactly happened to you?
I got shot out of a gun by an explosive bullet.
I'm almost tempted to make you walk around like that all the time.
Because I'm so hot?
Because you look so damn stupid.
Why does everyone think I'm stupid?
Space aliens thought I was cool once.
Hey, once, some scientist-guy thought Aaron would be useful.
Did you just hear gunshots?
nextWAVE
would like to remind the audience that dragging insane, corrupt police officers who change into giant killer robots into an alleyway and shooting them a lot is very bad and not the Marvel way. And also still illegal in most states.
End

NEXTWAVE
AGENTS OF H.A.T.E.
chapter five
H.A.T.E.
immonen.ca

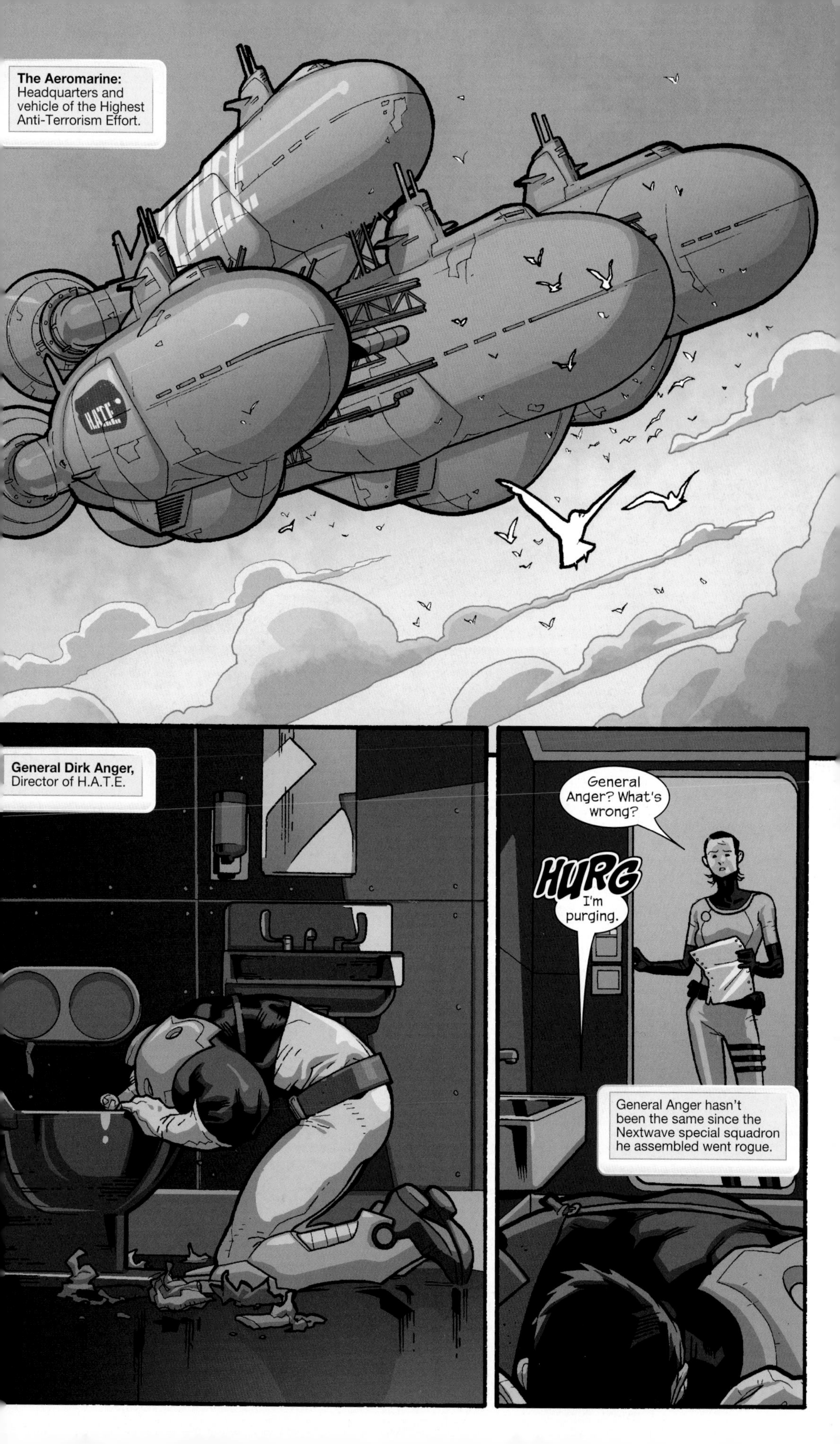

The Aeromarine: Headquarters and vehicle of the Highest Anti-Terrorism Effort.
H.A.T.E.
General Dirk Anger, Director of H.A.T.E.
General Anger? What's wrong?
HURG
I'm purging.
General Anger hasn't been the same since the Nextwave special squadron he assembled went rogue.

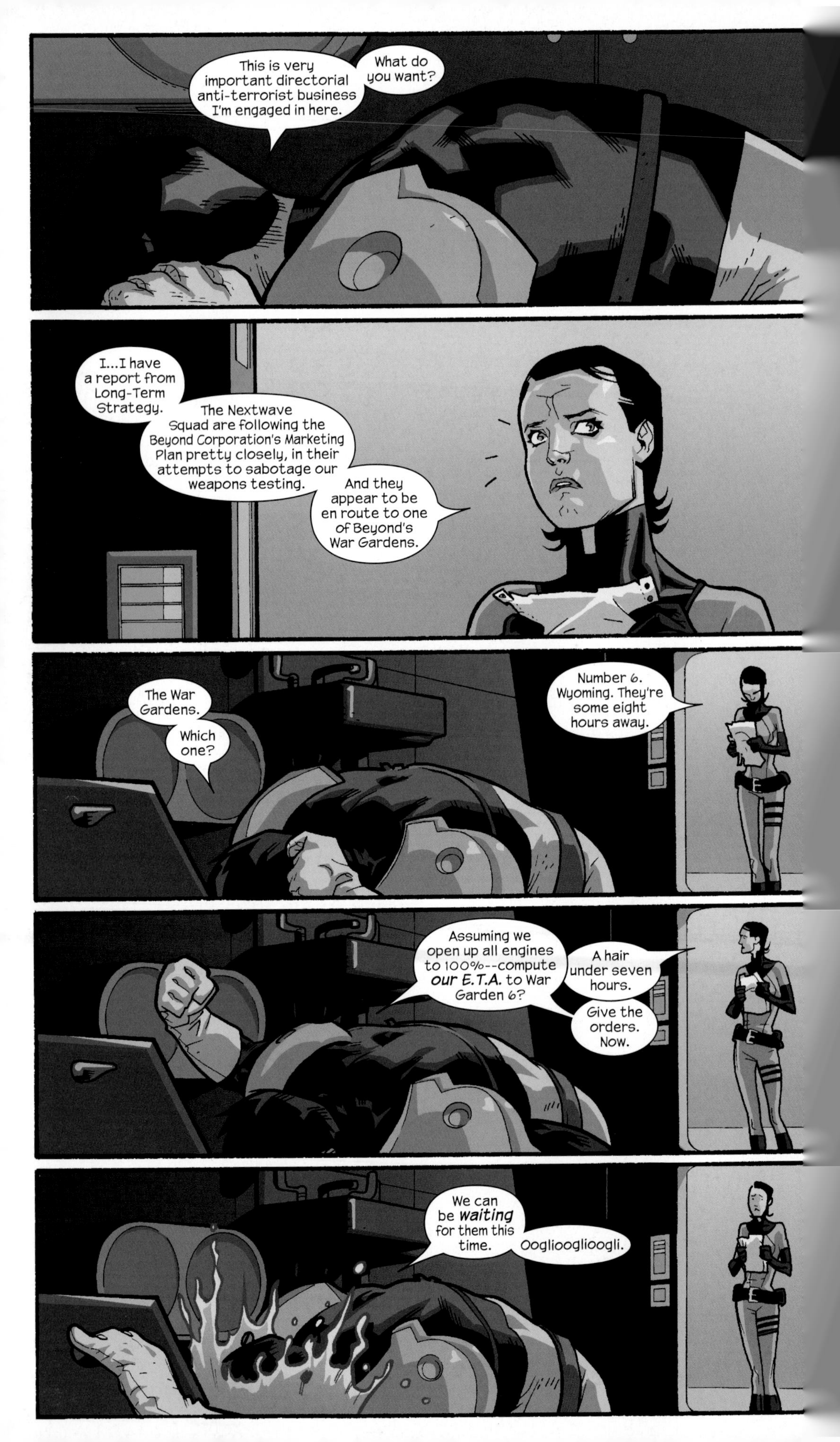
This is very important directorial anti-terrorist business I'm engaged in here.
What do you want?
I...I have a report from Long-Term Strategy.
The Nextwave Squad are following the Beyond Corporation's Marketing Plan pretty closely, in their attempts to sabotage our weapons testing.
And they appear to be en route to one of Beyond's War Gardens.
The War Gardens.
Which one?
Number 6. Wyoming. They're some eight hours away.
Assuming we open up all engines to 100%--compute our E.T.A. to War Garden 6?
A hair under seven hours.
Give the orders. Now.
We can be waiting for them this time.
Ooglioogliioogli.

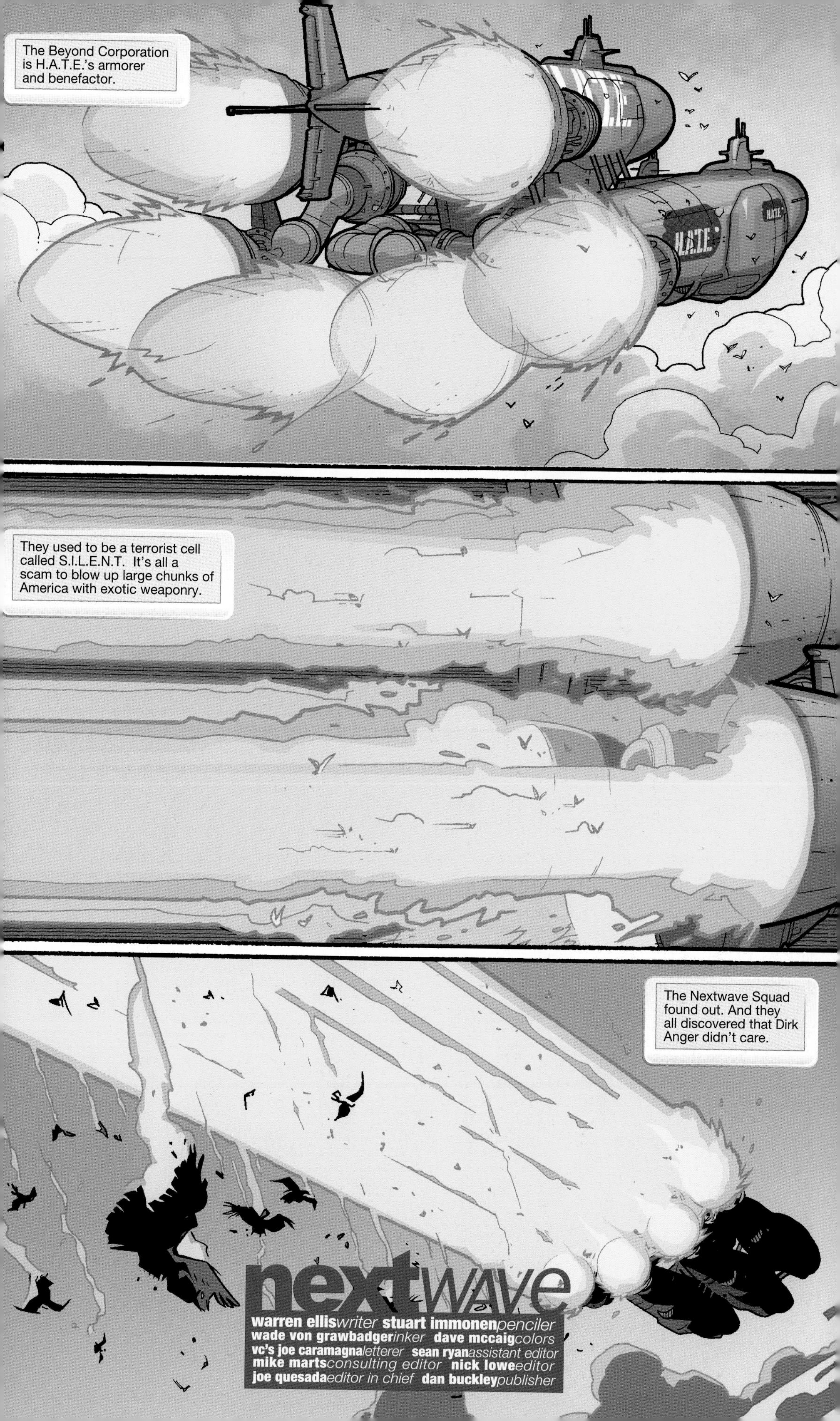
The Beyond Corporation is H.A.T.E.'s armorer and benefactor.
H.A.T.E.
They used to be a terrorist cell called S.I.L.E.N.T. It's all a scam to blow up large chunks of America with exotic weaponry.
The Nextwave Squad found out. And they all discovered that Dirk Anger didn't care.
nextWAVE
warren elliswriter stuart immonenpenciler
wade von grawbadgerinker dave mccaigcolors
vc's joe caramagnaletterer sean ryanassistant editor
mike martsconsulting editor nick loweeditor
joe quesadaeditor in chief dan buckleypublisher

The Shockwave Rider: Experimental vehicle stolen by the Nextwave Squad when they went rogue from H.A.T.E., after having swiped Beyond's planning documents.
So this is all owned by the Beyond Corporation?
As far as the eye can see, according to the Plan.
They call this a War Garden. I mean, God only knows what that means, but it sounded worth blowing up, right?
Holy hell.
...okay. That's worth blowing up.
Park us over it. We're going down to do som gardening.

Human Resources operatives.
They actually grow them. Like crops.
BATCH 73-42C

Seeing them like this...isn't it weird?
That they grow things that can, like, think, or react... that they grow things to try and kill us with.
Doesn't that seem really sad to you?
Sad. Sick.
God, it's quiet. This is so... uncomfortable, you know?
So what do we do?
We dig for victory darling.
You're not serious.
After all the trouble these nasty little men have given us?
You're ☠☠☠☠ right I'm serious.

Yick.
Perfectly horrid little people.
God, they stink like my mom's cooking.
Okay. The more of these things we uproot, the fewer there are to try and cap us next time we do a gig.
Slash and burn, people.
I'm sorry, broccoli murder-dudes. You just grow up to be, like, too harsh, you know?
I swear to God, nowhere on *Earth* do they talk like you, Tabby.
Come on, robot boy. Do some work.
You mean you don't?
Want I should do your laundry, too?

Shut up. I am a unique robot intellect.
You're ☠☠☠☠. I mean, you're the ☠☠☠☠ robot I ever heard of.
Aaron, I'm sorry, man, but you are a bit ☠☠☠☠.
Listen, you-- I was taken up into space by the Celestials because I'm so ☠☠☠☠ great.
Space gods. Interstellar travel. Everything.
So why'd you come back?
Aaron Stack, you who were called Machine Man. You have travelled with us for three hundred and sixty cycles by your reckoning of time.
There is now something we have to tell you.
You are total ☠☠☠☠.

What?
No. Really. You're ☠☠☠☠.
We've taken a year of you. We're taking you back to that orbiting trashcan you call a planet. And dumping you there.
You're turning away from us. We are speaking to you and you're turning away from us. This is exactly the kind of ☠☠☠☠ we were talking about here.
Please... don't look...
I don't want you to believe...
...that even a robot can cry.
See what we mean? Complete and utter ☠☠☠☠.
I decided I could do more good among you ☠☠☠☠ fleshy ones.
I will *slap* you if you keep calling us *"fleshy ones."*

Guys.
I think we may have a problem.
What?
My generic set of special super hero abilities includes a broader scale of vision.
There's something big out there, and pretty heavily electrified...
H.A.T.E.

Oh, ☠☠☠☠.
Deactivating invisibility cloud. All stations report Condition Stomp-Circle readiness.
Moo hoo ha ha.
CONDITION STOMP-CIRCLE!
DEPLOY THE ARMAGEDDON HORN!
What in hell is that?
I don't know. Scatter. Now.

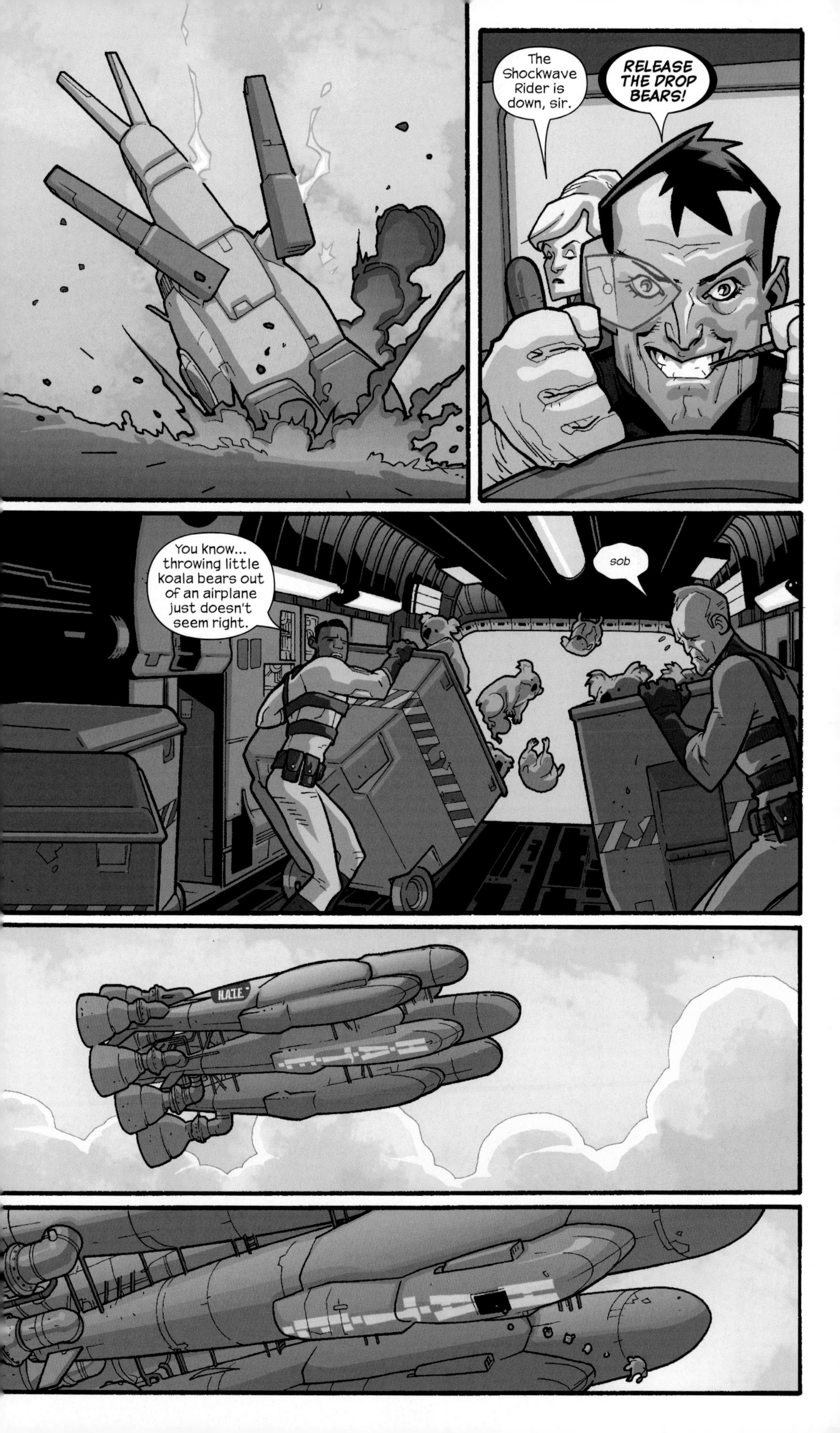
The Shockwave Rider is down, sir.
RELEASE THE DROP BEARS!
You know... throwing little koala bears out of an airplane just doesn't seem right.
sob
H.A.T.E.

What the--?
Awwwww. Widdle cuddly bears.
Dirk Anger's lost it. I mean, what? He chucks teddy bears out of his stupid flying boat and we're supposed to cry ourselves into submission?
Tabby, turn on your powers.
Aaron, go to combat status. Ellie, are you armed?
I've got two Uzis and a shovel.
Which, I suppose, means I can shoot things and bury them afterwards.
Widdle cuddly bears... of *death*?

AAAAAAAA! DEATH BEARS!
Suffer, fleshy ones.
Ha. Fear my robot head.
Aaron, help them.
<burst of white noise as Monica turns into 120 pounds of photons>
Monica Rambeau appears to be in the air, sir.
Excellent. Give the drop order to...
...the Assault Pterosuit Flock.
The order's given. Start chewin', soldiers.
You are men. You have guns. You chew Lizard Boom Sticks.

And you wear Combat Pterodactyl Suits.
Oh, God, now what...
We didn't have to deal with this kind of thing in the Avengers.
It's the Gamma-Activated Bull Men From Beyond The Nineteenth Perimeter--
--and they're naked.
Cover your eyes, go back to Avengers Mansion, and make my dinner.
Monica Rambeau, leader of the Nextwave Squad, lies all the time.

They're not *bullets!* They're *Quantum-Tunnel Drill Bits!*
They're verywhere and where, existing in all states at once!
They can even kill someone who's converted their mass to *photons!*
Schrödinger's death!

I hate teddy bears.
The
had as
a
as any of
Nextwave
...Special Bear?
Special Bear's dead.
Aaron! Make yourself useful!
You'll be sorry, fleshy one.
This is a nightmare.

Oh my God.
I just shot koalas.
Ow ow OW don't cut me!
Quit moving or I'll let the bears eat you.
No no NO bears not eat me!
Monica's in ouble. Aaron nd I should rovide some air support for her...
...Oh, what now?
H.A.T.E.
H.A.T.E.
H.A.T.E.

Yes!
Yes!
Samuroid Batch 23!
SAMUROID BATCH 23!
Samurai robots beat guns. No question.
So it's just me and a shovel.
Rock.

Not just you.
Cap, Aaron-- you need to stop the Aeromarine from throwing all this sick junk at us.
Me and English girl have got this one covered.
You ready for this?
Hey, English girl, I used to do business with Cable and X-Force, you know what I'm saying?
Tabitha! Quickly! To *me*, my X-bait!
Help me lift my *gun!* Techno-organic prolapse *imminent!*
I've had to handle worse things than robots with big swords.
Tick tick tick **BOOM.**
Your sci-fi kung fu bullets are not strong.
Infrared Stab.

AAAAAAA
First blood! *First blood!*
You laughed at me. You *laughed!*
You should have been ☠☠☠☠ begging me not to kill you!
you have been reading nextWAVE
To be continued...

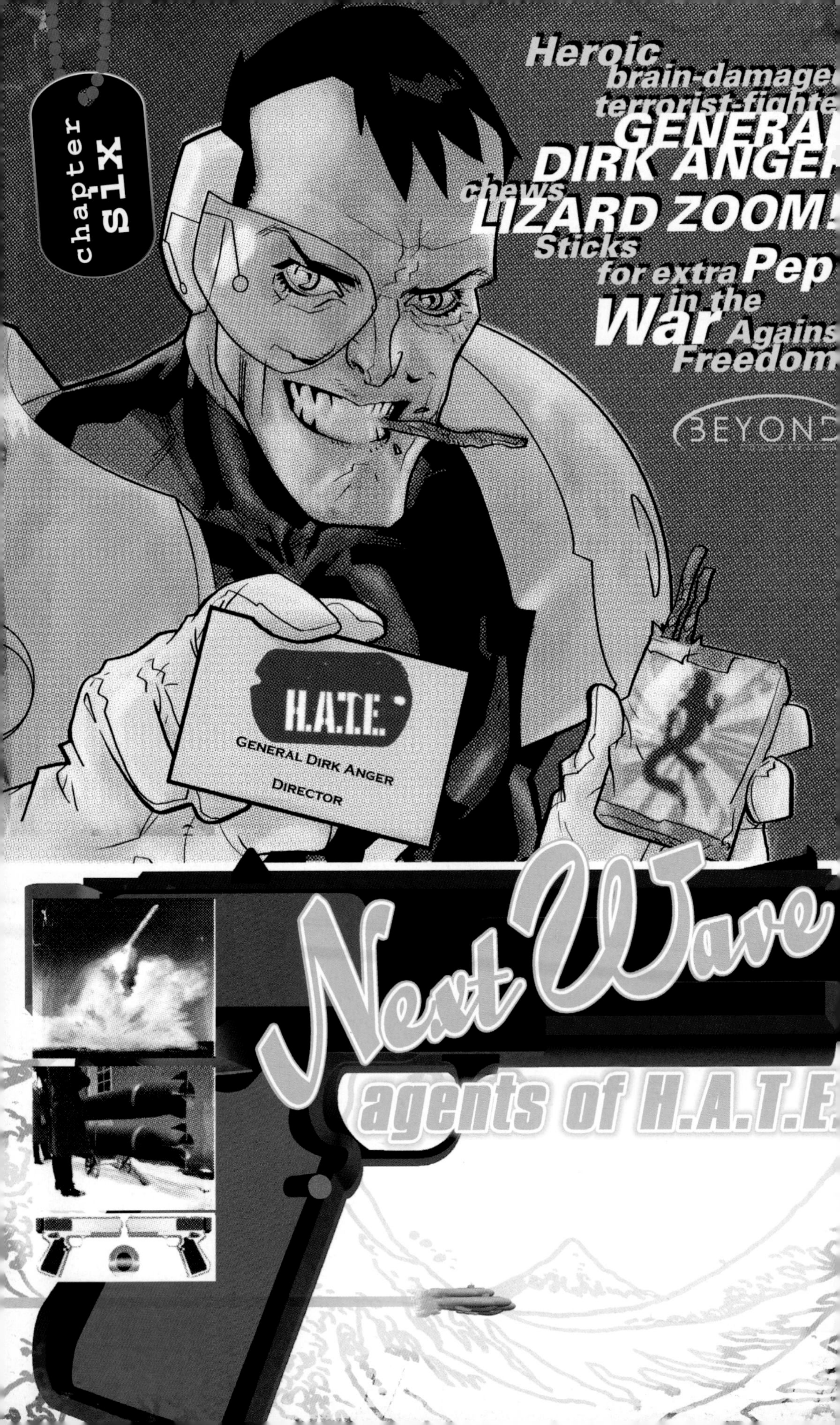
chapter six
Heroic
brain-damage
terrorist-fighte
GENERA
DIRK ANGE
chews
LIZARD ZOOM!
Sticks
for extra Pep
in the
War Agains
Freedom
BEYOND
H.A.T.E.
GENERAL DIRK ANGER
DIRECTOR
Next Wave
agents of H.A.T.E.

I make it six each.
Don't you try and impress me with your English counting. You KNOW I growed up in a trailer park.
Let's just kill 'em.
nextwave
ren elliswriter stuart immonenpenciler
e von grawbadgerinker dave mccaigcolors
joe caramagnaletterer sean ryanassistant editor
e martsconsulting editor nick loweeditor
quesadaeditor in chief dan buckleypublisher

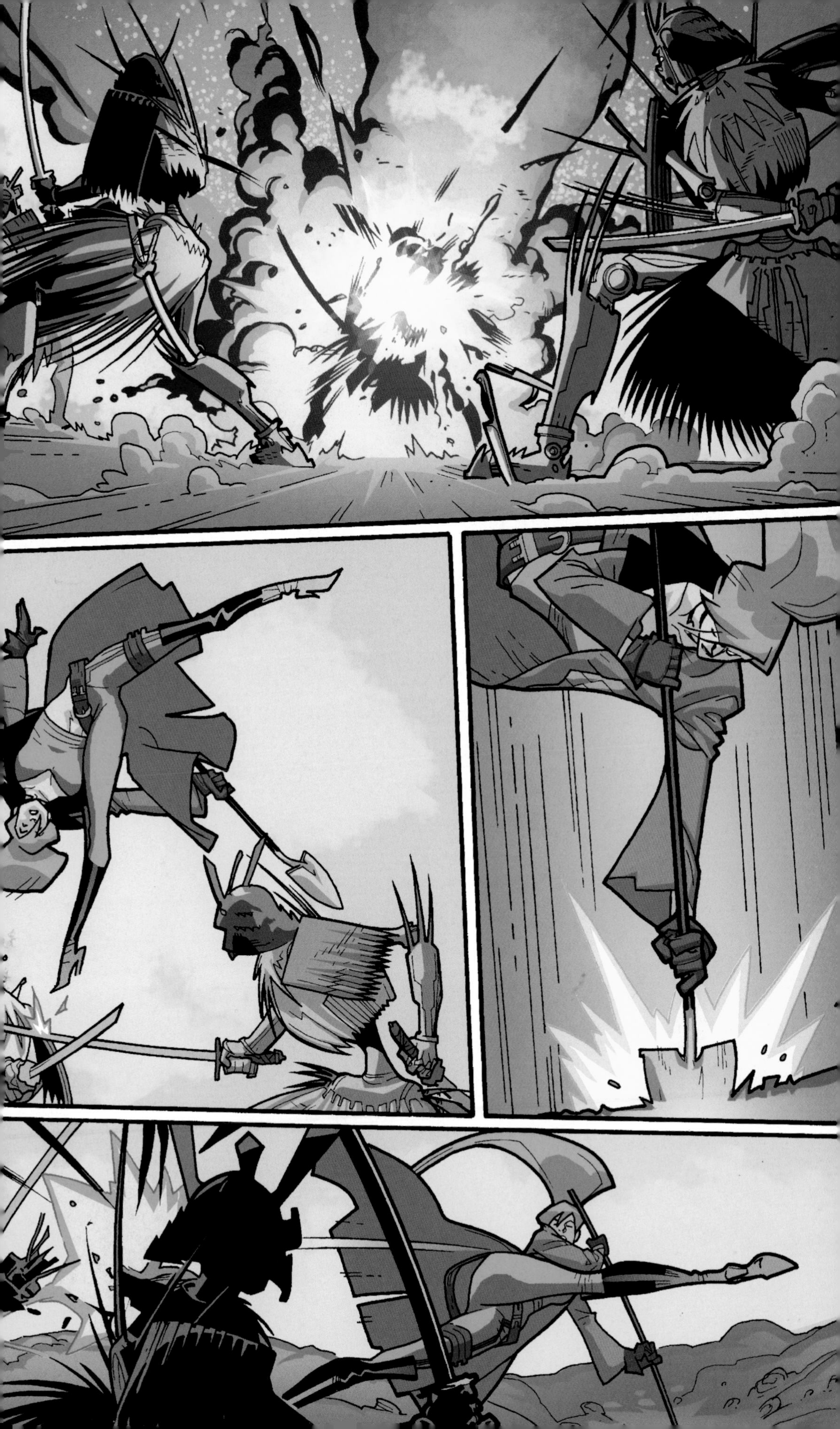

That's it. I tried to do the whole nonlethal thing.
But now you've *shot* me, I don't care so much.
Ultraviolet Nova.

NO! My beautiful Pteromen!
That's *it!*
I wanted to ***play*** with you! I wanted to ***torture*** you!
But ***YOU ALWAYS FIND A WAY TO SPOIL MY FUN!***

You know who you are? You know what you're like? You're just like my *wife!*
That's *right!*
Everything was fine and dandy, and then I ask you to do *one little thing!*
What did I say to you, Monica? I mean, what was so *awful* about it?
I said perform the weapons tests and don't worry your little girly head about the weapons coming from a company that used to be a terrorist cell!
I said blow up chunks of America for *freedom!*
But *no!* You *couldn't!*
ONE LITTLE THING!
It's like you suddenly turned *forty* and your *face* went south and suddenly it was no, *Dirk*, I *won't* do those things with the chickens and the wig and the bath full of acid for you any more!
And by the *way*, Dirk, give me all your *cash*, let me paint everything *pink*, adopt a million screaming little snot-factory *children* for me and don't you *dare* touch me or my *womb* will fall out!

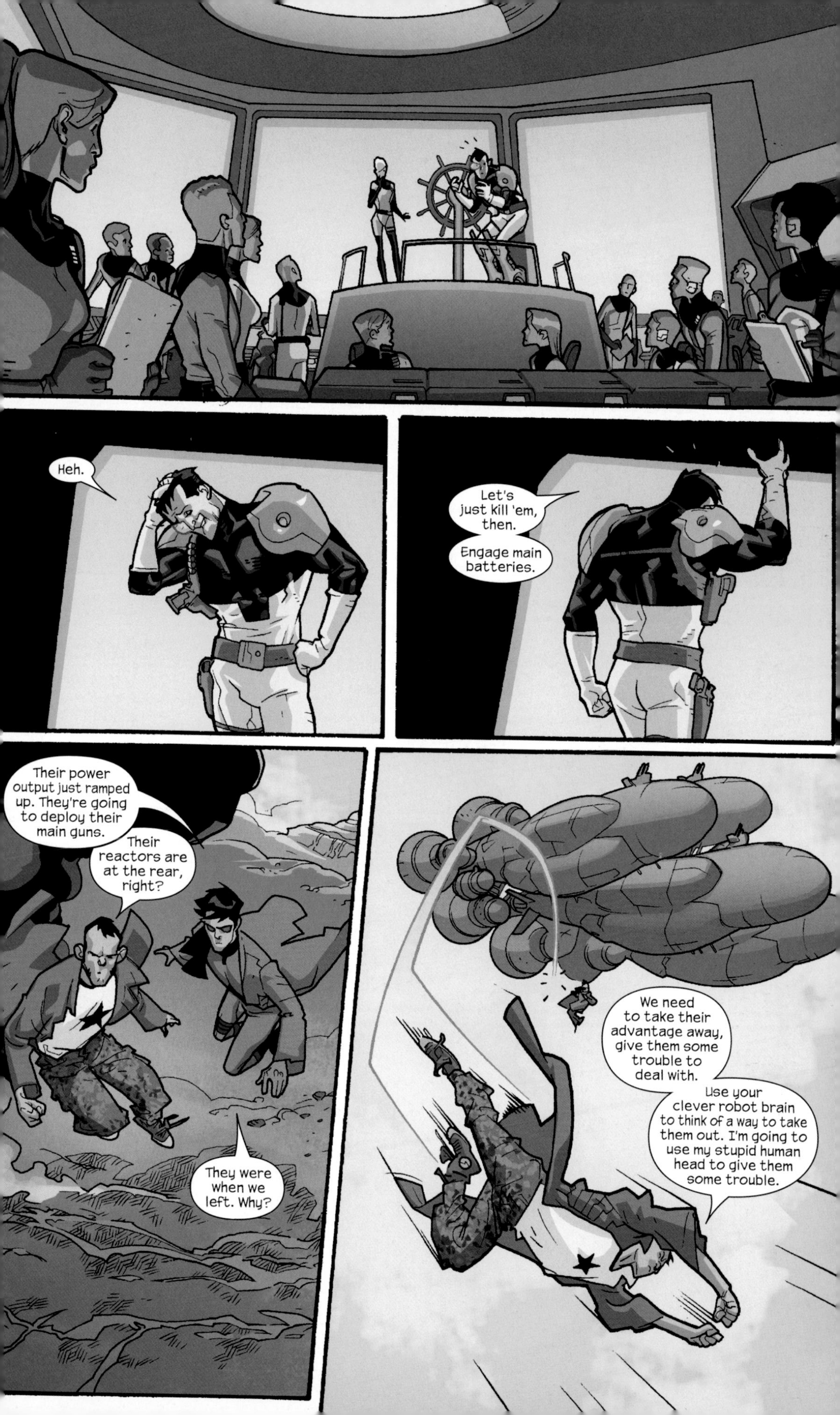
Heh.
Let's just kill 'em, then.
Engage main batteries.
Their power output just ramped up. They're going to deploy their main guns.
Their reactors are at the rear, right?
They were when we left. Why?
We need to take their advantage away, give them some trouble to deal with.
Use your clever robot brain to think of a way to take them out. I'm going to use my stupid human head to give them some trouble.

Those are some big ☠☠☠☠ guns.
PETAWATT LASER!

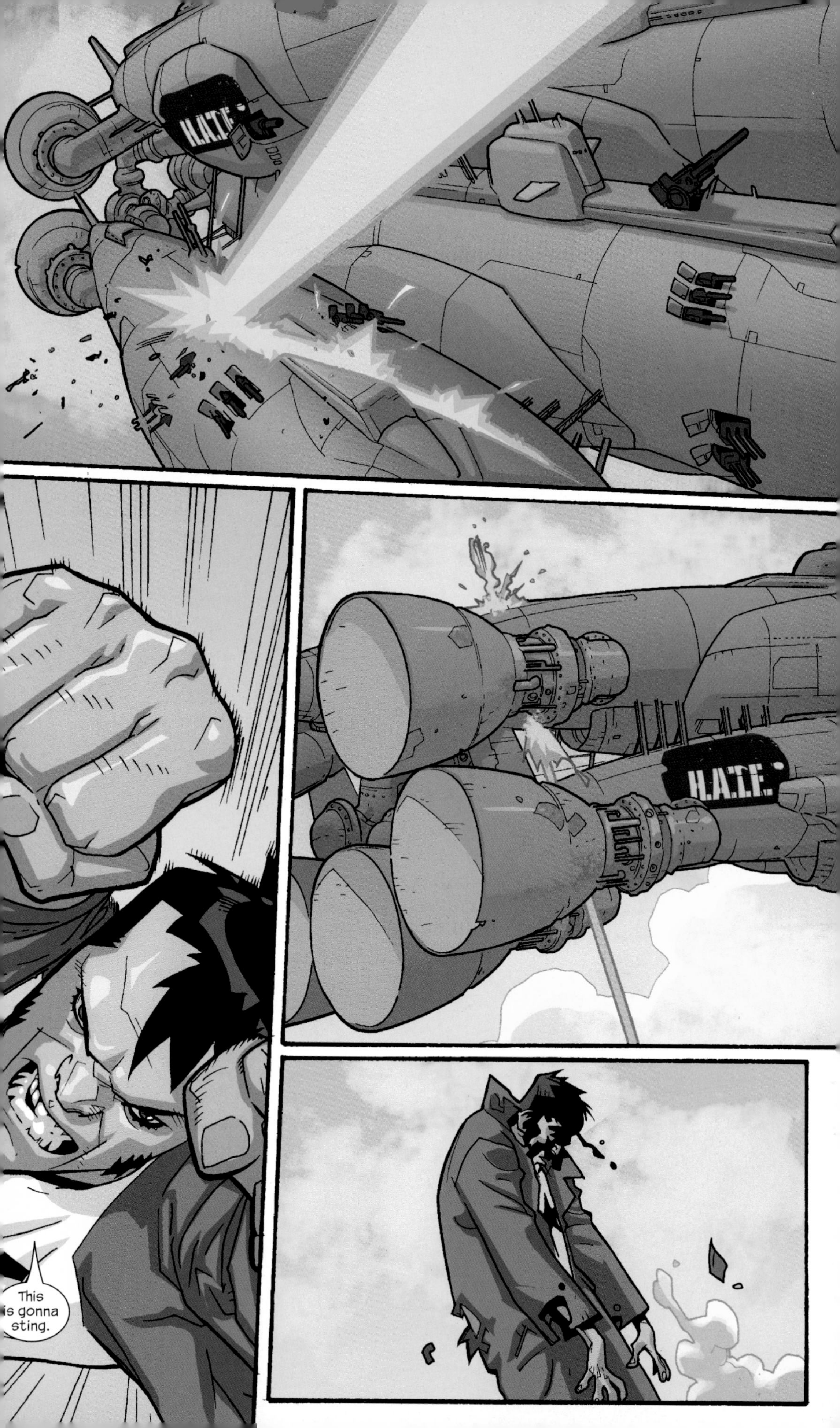
H.A.T.E.
H.A.T.E.
This is gonna sting.

I own.

Go boom now.

Sir, there's trouble in the reactor feed to engine two--
I don't care! Forty-degr declination! We're g to fire the remain batteries right a those three on the ground!

My robot brain is *superior.*
It is not ☠☠☠☠ at all.
I remember everything. Even the things I'm not supposed to know.
And I know how to end this.
...ah.

Let's remind Dirk who he's dealing with.
AAAAAA!
What in the name of Satan's ancient underpants is going on?
This is Monica Rambeau. I'm on the hull. I just flooded the Aeromarine with X-rays.
That was a quick burst. A long burst will leave all of you with permanent cell damage.
Back off, Dirk.
Like hell!
HOMICIDE CRABS!

C'mere,
fleshy one.

No more mister nice robot.
This is getting silly now.

This is ridiculous. They're just going to throw something else at us now.
They'll beat us down in waves unless we do something drastic.
You think Cap's dead?
He's a guy. How would you be able to tell?
Well, he wouldn't be farting.
Gen. D. Anger
PRIVATE QUARTERS
Ah, yes. Many was the night I'd sneak in here to steal his beer.
Until I found out he made the beer himself.
And what he made it out of.
I thought "Lizard Squeezings" was a brewery name.

Release the NEO-HYDE GUTSPAWN!
Human scum empowered by the cloned chemically-mutated cells found in the stomach walls of the corpse of Henry Jekyll himself!
They eat girls, Monica! Ha ha ha ha ha! THEY EAT GIRLS!
Put the Atomic Puppies in the torpedo tubes!
Yap yap bang! Ha ha ha ha ha!
YAP YAP BANG!
Dirk Anger!
Direct your hull cameras directly in front of the Aeromarine's prow!
I have something to show you!
Do you see it?

yes

Give us your word that you'll turn and leave, and I will replace this object.
Press your attack and I will incinerate the dress.

please
please don't do this
just let me kill you

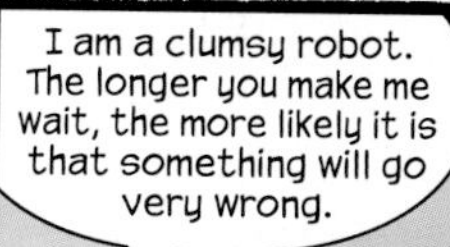

I am a clumsy robot. The longer you make me wait, the more likely it is that something will go very wrong.
Oops. My blowtorch unit just lit.
It was an accident. I am sorry.

...give the order.
Sir.
Stand down, dammit.

But sir, we've got them where we want them, how can some old dress--
STAND. DOWN.

Is Cap dead?
He's farting.
Okay.
What the hell?
I gave him back the dress. I borrowed some other stuff.
Stop looking at my chest, fleshy one.
I have saved the day.
I think I'm going to throw up.
Bow down, hoo-ma "friends." I am not ☠☠☠☠ robot. I Aaron Stack, her robot, and you can bite my valve.
Why is the ☠☠☠☠ robot wearing one of Andrea Dworkin's old bras?
Who?
Okay, now I'm definitely going to throw up. Thank you all.

Our ride's pretty messed up, guys.
I can get the thing running again. It's packed full of repair gear.
I don't know if it'll ever be the same, but it'll fly again.
Aaron, take that off. It's just ☠☠☠☠ing disturbing, darling.
Lick my blinky diodes. I'm the hero today.
nextwave
is love

It's not all right.
It will never be
all right again.
Nothing will ever
be the same.
No good can
come of a robot
in a bra.
you have been reading
nextWAVE

The Nextwave Original Pitch

This is a "remix" book. The Next Wave was actually the name of a crap Marvel supervillain group in the 80s. All the protagonists are old Marvel characters or carry old Marvel trademark names.

The quasi-governmental security and defense organisation H.A.T.E. — Highest Anti-Terrorism Effort — bought the rights to the name, and Dirk Anger, Director Of H.A.T.E., recruited five troubled, obscure super heroes to form The Next Wave Squad, an elite intervention force in the War On Terrorism:

MONICA RAMBEAU used to be known as Captain Marvel. She once ran the Avengers. She will tell you this. A lot. An unlikely veteran of superhuman combat, wanting to do her bit for her country, she found herself leading this team. AARON STACK used to be called Machine Man, but his name is Aaron Stack, and it's none of your business that he's wired his robot brain to be affected by alcohol. ELSA BLOODSTONE is the daughter of near-immortal monster hunter Ulysses Bloodstone, wears the same creepy gem that makes her superhumanly resistant to harm, works in the family business and tends to come off like Lara Croft's evil twin sister. THE CAPTAIN claims not to remember his real name – his chequered career has seen him basically be every crap Marvel character called Captain something. TABITHA SMITH used to be Boom Boom in the New Mutants and Meltdown in X-Force, and she's a terrible kleptomaniac, and it's because of her light fingers that The Next Wave Squad discovered that...

...well, it seems that H.A.T.E. isn't fighting the same war on terrorism as everyone else.

They are funded and supplied by a multinational called The Beyond Corporation, and much of their time seems to be taken on testing and deploying weapons. The Beyond Corp used to be a terrorist cell called S.I.L.E.N.T. In an open bidding process, they have co-opted their opponents to test their own Unusual Weapons Of Mass Destruction.

This is all laid out in the Beyond Corp's Marketing Plan, which the Next Wave Squad have stolen. Along with The Shockwave Rider, an experimental assault plane with an inexhaustible power supply. Nextwave have gone rogue with the blueprint for Beyond's plan to devastate a series of American towns in a product-testing process.

For instance; digging the 150-foot atomic monster in purple underpants Fin Fang Foom out of his hibernation sac inside a mountain overlooking the town of Abcess, North Dakota.

Nextwave have that to cope with. And the Beyond Corp Human Resources Department, an army of plant-human freaks in red three-piece suits and Dr Doom armor. And, of course, H.A.T.E., with their goofy Sixties-Steranko technology, and their immense flying Aeromarine, four massive submarines nailed together with girders and plastic tunnels.

Dirk Anger is slowly having a massive nervous breakdown. He thinks no-one can tell.

Two-issue story arcs – every two months, a complete story, and then on to the next threat on the list, or the next trap H.A.T.E. set for them. One story-arc makes a European book. Three makes a TPB. Six make an Absolute-style book. Early storylines include, yes, the return of Fin Fang Foom;

NEXTWAVE is not about Character Arcs and Learning and Morals and Hugs. It is about cramming an insane movie into 44 pages at a time. It is about the mad things underpinning Marvel Comics – SHIELD ****, **** – and it is about special effects out of Asian cinema and absurd levels of destruction and a skewed sense of humour and Spectacle and things blowing up and people getting kicked.

It is most especially about THINGS BLOWING UP and PEOPLE GETTING KICKED.

It is about humanoid Clone Things made out of engine oil and broccoli being smacked to death by a woman with a guitar.

NEXTWAVE. Healing America by beating people up.

— **W**

NEXTWAVE

...theme song
......by Thunder Thighs

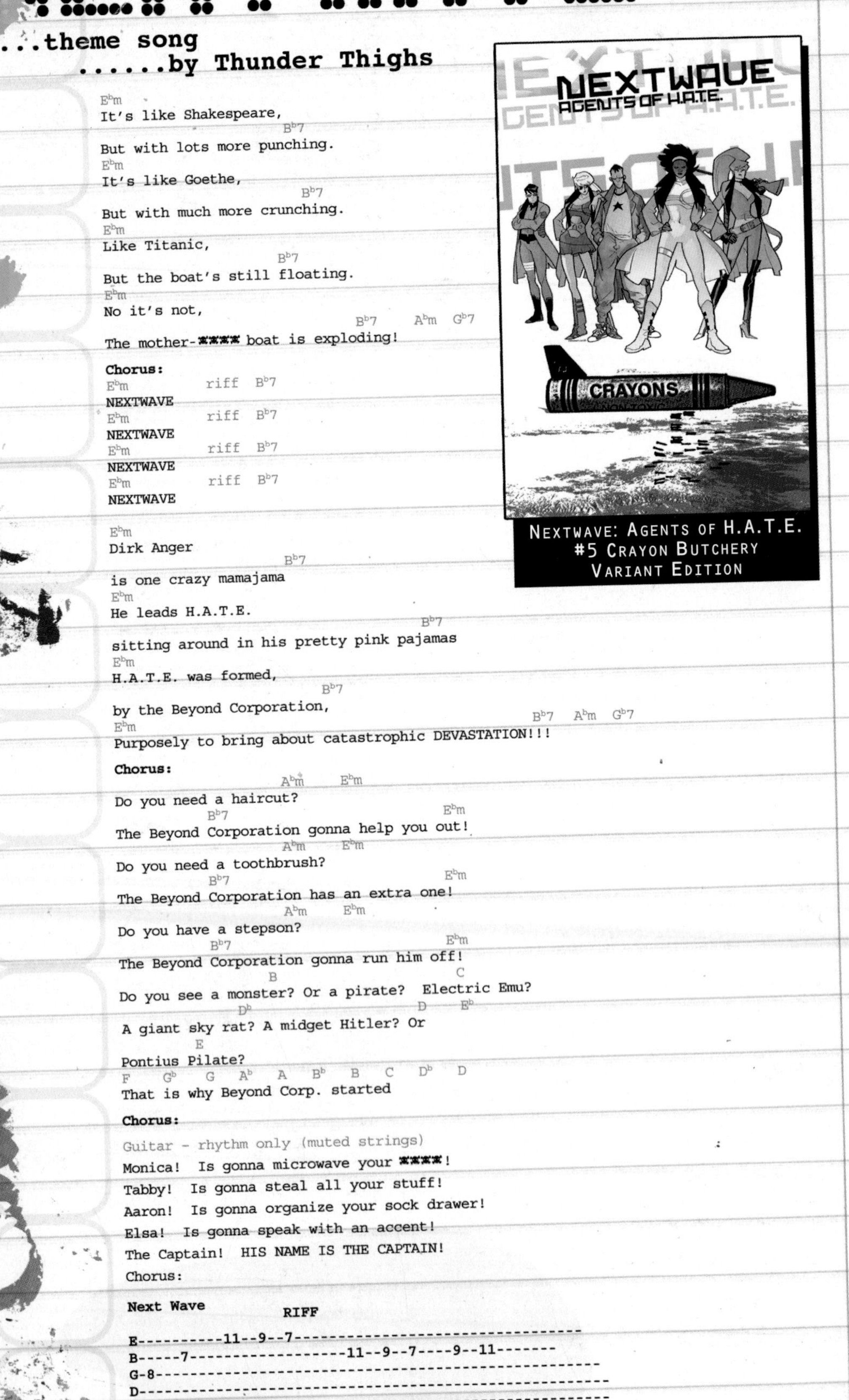

Nextwave: Agents of H.A.T.E.
#5 Crayon Butchery
Variant Edition

```
Ebm
It's like Shakespeare,
                    Bb7
But with lots more punching.
Ebm
It's like Goethe,
                      Bb7
But with much more crunching.
Ebm
Like Titanic,
                   Bb7
But the boat's still floating.
Ebm
No it's not,
                          Bb7    Abm  Gb7
The mother-**** boat is exploding!
```

Chorus:

```
Ebm        riff  Bb7
NEXTWAVE
Ebm        riff  Bb7
NEXTWAVE
Ebm        riff  Bb7
NEXTWAVE
Ebm        riff  Bb7
NEXTWAVE
```

```
Ebm
Dirk Anger
                 Bb7
is one crazy mamajama
Ebm
He leads H.A.T.E.
                                Bb7
sitting around in his pretty pink pajamas
Ebm
H.A.T.E. was formed,
                    Bb7
by the Beyond Corporation,
Ebm                                            Bb7  Abm  G b7
Purposely to bring about catastrophic DEVASTATION!!!
```

Chorus:

```
                 Abm    Ebm
Do you need a haircut?
             Bb7                  Ebm
The Beyond Corporation gonna help you out!
                 Abm    Ebm
Do you need a toothbrush?
             Bb7                  Ebm
The Beyond Corporation has an extra one!
                 Abm    Ebm
Do you have a stepson?
             Bb7                  Ebm
The Beyond Corporation gonna run him off!
                 B                   C
Do you see a monster? Or a pirate?  Electric Emu?
               Db                D    Eb
A giant sky rat? A midget Hitler? Or
           E
Pontius Pilate?
F   Gb   G  Ab  A   Bb  B  C  Db  D
That is why Beyond Corp. started
```

Chorus:

Guitar - rhythm only (muted strings)
Monica! Is gonna microwave your **!**
Tabby! Is gonna steal all your stuff!
Aaron! Is gonna organize your sock drawer!
Elsa! Is gonna speak with an accent!
The Captain! HIS NAME IS THE CAPTAIN!
Chorus:

Next Wave **RIFF**

```
E----------11--9--7--------------------------------
B-----7------------------11--9--7----9--11-------
G-8---------------------------------------------------
D-----------------------------------------------------
A-----------------------------------------------------
E-----------------------------------------------------
```